W9-ANY-480

Young Believer on Tour

Noah

Stephen Arterburn
with Angela Hunt

TYNDALE KiDS

Tyndale House Publishers, Inc.
Wheaton, Illinois

Visit Tyndale's exciting Web site at www.tyndale.com

Visit the Young Believer Web site at www.youngbeliever.com

Copyright © 2004 by Stephen Arterburn and Angela Elwell Hunt. All rights reserved.

Cover illustration copyright © 2004 by Juan Alvarez. All rights reserved.

Published by Tyndale House Publishers in association with the literary agency of Alive
Communications, Inc., 7680 Goddard Street, Suite 200, Colorado Springs, Colorado 80920.
All rights reserved. No part of this book may be reproduced, stored in a retrieval system,
or transmitted in any form or by any other means—electronic, mechanical, photocopy,
recording, or any other—except for brief quotations in printed reviews, without prior
permission from the publisher.

Scripture quotations are taken from the *Holy Bible*, New Living Translation, copyright ©
1996. Used by permission of Tyndale House Publishers, Inc., Wheaton, Illinois 60189. All
rights reserved.

RC's animal stories in chapter 23 were adapted from P. L. Tan's *Encyclopedia of 7700
Illustrations: A Treasury of Illustrations, Anecdotes, Facts and Quotations for Pastors,
Teachers and Christian Workers* (Garland, Tex.: Bible Communications, 1979).

This novel is a work of fiction. Names, characters, places, and incidents are either the
product of the author's imagination or are used fictitiously. Any resemblance to actual
events, locales, organizations or persons, living or dead, is entirely coincidental and
beyond the intent of either the author or the publisher.

Library of Congress Cataloging-in-Publication Data

Arterburn, Stephen.
  Noah / Stephen Arterburn and Angela Elwell Hunt.
    p. cm. — (Young believer on tour ; 3)
  Summary: When approached by the father who abandoned him and his mother years
earlier, Noah discovers that forgiveness comes at a price and, in the meantime, he
struggles to figure out how to deal with Paige's crush on him.
  ISBN 0-8423-8337-9 (sc)
  [1. Forgiveness—Fiction. 2. Fathers and sons—Fiction. 3. Interpersonal relations—
Fiction. 4. Musical groups—Fiction. 5. Christian life—Fiction.] I. Hunt, Angela Elwell.
II. Title.
  PZ7.A74357No 2004
  [Fic]—dc22   2003023522

Printed in the United States of America

10 09 08 07 06 05 04
7   6   5   4   3   2   1

Some people ask us why we spend our time,

Singing songs with occasional retro themes,

They can't seem to feel the rhythm and rhyme,

There's an ancient pulse behind everything,

Life's greatest gifts are as old as the sky,

Love and laughter come to us from above,

Every good and great thing that meets the eye,

Spills from the bounty of the Father's love.

—Paige Clawson and Shane Clawson

FROM "COME ON (IT'S TIME TO TAKE YOUR STAND)"
YB2 MUSIC, INC.

September 30

YB2 CONCERT DOESN'T DISAPPOINT

By Mandi Tanner, Fanzine News Coverage

National pop sensations YB2 (Young Believers, Second Edition) gave their young fans a taste of their new album last week—and left the crowd hungry for more. Singing to a capacity crowd at Columbus's Nationwide Arena, teen idols Paige and Shane Clawson, Noah Dudash, Liane Nelson, and newcomer Josiah Johnson presented a dynamic show featuring songs from their upcoming CD, *Never Stop Believin'*.

The young singers performed before a crowd of more than 15,000 fans and a squadron of camera operators filming the event for a Nickelodeon TV special. The crowd waited patiently through a twenty-minute delay that prevented an on-time start, but the moment YB2 took the stage, all was forgiven.

This performance demonstrated how far the quintet has come since the debut of their self-titled first album last year, and spotlighted the talent of their newest addition, tenor Josiah Johnson from Roanoke, Virginia. With the songs from *Never Stop Believin'*, they have expanded their sound to include even more boy-band-style dance pop—but keep in mind, of course, that YB2 features two girls, Paige Clawson and Liane Nelson, both of whom are exceptional vocalists. Paige Clawson, who conceals her blindness behind dark glasses, is the keyboardist and co-composer of many of the group's songs. Her brother, Shane, is the group's main heartthrob, whose talent is as undeniable as his teen idol status.

Ron Clawson, founder of the group and father to Paige and Shane, has made tremendous strides in pushing both the group's popularity and its artistic appeal.

The "Never Stop Believin'" tour features energetic choreography that's more fun to watch than many comparable groups. The new song "Livin' in Futurisity" is a tribute to the rapid changes brought on by technology, and the robot-like costumes are a great touch to a unique number.

YB2 LIVE in Columbus will air on Nickelodeon in November. Be sure to tune in—the concert is something the entire family will enjoy.

Noah

Even through the heavy curtain of sleep, Noah Dudash felt the bus turn left, then right, then left again. They never made sharp turns on the interstate, which meant they had to be . . . home!

He was dreaming of a summer picnic outside the YB2 house when the deep growl of the diesel engines abruptly ceased. The dream of steaming apple pie vanished, replaced by the shadowy outline of the bunk only a few inches from his nose.

He lifted his head and blinked. "Are we home?"

Across the aisle, Shane Clawson rolled out of his bunk. "Yes, we are! Hel-loooooo, Aunt Rhonda!"

While Shane sprinted down the aisle toward the door, Noah propped himself onto one elbow, then pressed his hand to the canvas bunk overhead. "Hey, Joe, wake up. We're home, dude."

Noah

"Huh?"

"Time to roll out. RC will want us to unload the luggage."

A moment later Josiah Johnson's bleary eyes peered over the edge of the bunk. "We're already back in Orlando?"

"Larry drove all night, man. So yeah, let's unload the luggage and then take a dip in the pool. It'll feel good to stretch out a little."

Across the aisle, Liane Nelson groaned and rolled out of her bunk. Beneath her Paige Clawson, by far the group's heaviest sleeper, kept snoring.

They hadn't been home since mid-September, when their schedule had allowed them to take a two-day break in Orlando after performing at the Latin Grammy Awards show in Miami. After a quick break at their home base, they had boarded the bus for a tour through the Northeast and into Toronto, Canada, where they had been featured during the broadcast of Canada's MuchMusic Video Awards show. After their performance, Noah had been astonished when YB2 received the award for "Favourite International Group" from the Canadians.

They'd all been excited to receive the honor, but they'd had no time to celebrate. From Toronto they'd traveled to Boston for a performance, then to concerts in Manhattan, Chicago, and Detroit. They'd performed in a few smaller towns on their journey, but by the end of September, Noah had lost track of where they were. One civic center looked pretty much like another, and the hordes of screaming fans were alike from California to Maine.

Some time in Orlando, their home base, would be a welcome relief. RC had promised them the weekend off, plus he'd said they had a surprise waiting at the office. After the excitement of winning the Canadian award, Noah couldn't imagine what else RC had up his sleeve.

He glanced at his watch as he stood and moved down the aisle. Though it was barely seven-thirty, the sun had risen and the air outside the bus shimmered with heat. He pulled his sneakers from the overhead bin, then grabbed his book bag.

"Thanks, Larry." Noah caught the bus driver's eye in the rearview mirror as he headed for the door. "You must have made great time last night."

"No problem, dude." Larry stood from behind the wheel and hitched up his belt. "You guys have a good day, now. I'm picking up my car and heading to the motel to get some shut-eye."

Noah grinned. When they came back for brief breaks, Larry usually parked the bus around back and stayed in the guesthouse by the pool—but when he knew the team had a day off, he headed to the nearest motel instead. Experience had proved that he couldn't sleep while the YB2 guys were anywhere near the pool.

Noah was more than ready for a day off. He loved performing with YB2. He even loved the long hours of rehearsal, but doing the same thing day after day could get old. Touring held its challenges, and one of them was boredom. After a while, the miles of asphalt highway began to look alike.

Right now he'd give his right arm for an hour to be bored by the pool, maybe with a volleyball by his side. Shane and Liane and Josiah and Taz would almost definitely be up for a game of pool volleyball, and Paige would sit in the shallows and scream out encouragement for whichever team was losing.

Too bad she'd been born blind. She'd make a great competitor.

Noah stepped onto the paved driveway in his stockinged feet, then walked toward the double front doors with long strides. He didn't have to ring the bell, because Shane had already entered and announced their arrival. As Noah approached, one of the doors flew open. Rhonda Clawson, office manager and official "aunt" to all the team members, stepped onto the tiled porch with her arms open wide.

"Noah, my boy," she cried, wrapping him in a warm embrace. "Welcome back!"

"Thanks!" He dropped his book bag and shoes, then hugged her, breathing in the clean scents of soap and shampoo. He and the others probably smelled like dirty socks. They'd piled on the bus last night right after the concert in Jacksonville, and no one had cleaned up since.

She patted him on the back, then released him. "Go on inside—there's juice and doughnuts in the kitchen. Mail's on the foyer table, and something special is waiting in the family room."

He looked at her, hoping for some clue to the secret, but she had already moved past him on her way to greet Paige and Taz, YB2's sound engineer. Noah scooped up his book bag and shoes and hurried through the foyer, then walked past the waiting mail and food in the kitchen.

He wanted to know about the surprise.

He didn't see anything unusual when he first entered the large family room, then he saw a box on the coffee table. "Never Stop Believin'" had been stamped onto the side, and the words rattled in his brain for a full ten seconds before the realization hit—

"Our album!"

Dropping his shoes and book bag, Noah ran forward and opened the box. Stacks of freshly sealed, shiny CDs had been packed inside—YB2's second album, recorded in mid-August and now available in stores around the world.

"Wow." He sank to the edge of the sofa as his knees went weak. This was his second CD with YB2, but holding a new one in his hands still gave him goose bumps.

The others weren't far behind him. He had just turned the CD over and was reading the back credits when Liane and Josiah ran into the room, followed by Paige and Taz. Shane appeared an instant later, a glazed doughnut in his hand.

Liane caught Noah's eye. "Is that what I think it is?"

"Our album?"

"It's finally here!"

Grinning, Noah reached into the box and frisbeed other CDs to Shane, Liane, Taz, and Josiah. He waited until Paige had reached the couch, then reached out and placed one in her outstretched hand. "It's here," he said, bending her fingers around the cellophane-wrapped plastic. "And it's beautiful."

Paige's lips curled into a smile as the corners of her eyes lifted. "Cool," she whispered.

"Yeah," Noah agreed. "It's something special, isn't it?"

And as incredible as this CD seemed to Noah, he knew it had to feel even more amazing to Paige and Shane and RC. The group had performed all the songs on the CD, but Shane, Paige, and RC had written and arranged most of them. Noah sank back onto the sofa, boggled by the thought.

RC came through the doorway a moment later, his arm draped around his sister, Rhonda. He grinned at her. "I see they found the surprise."

"Yeah." She nodded. "But that's only half of my surprise. Yes, the new album is here, but here's the *really* good news—late last night I learned that presales were so high, the RIAA has already declared the album platinum!"

While the girls squealed, Josiah looked at Noah. "What's RIAA?"

Noah grinned. "The Recording Industry Association of America. You know what this means?"

Josiah shrugged. "So this is good, right?"

Aunt Rhonda answered for Noah. "You bet it's good. And it also means that tonight we're going out to celebrate. Take the afternoon off, everyone, but we've got to leave by six o'clock to make our reservations at the Bistro."

Liane's hand fluttered to her heart. "The *Bistro?* I love that place!"

"What's the Bistro?" Noah looked to RC. "Sounds fancy."

The director smiled. "It's Orlando's only revolving rooftop restaurant, and the view is spectacular. You can see Disney World, Universal Studios, SeaWorld—everything for miles. We'll be forty-four stories up."

Noah lifted a brow. He usually didn't care where they ate, but this place did sound nice. He could think of only one problem . . .

RC must have been thinking the same thing. "About these reservations . . ." He turned to face his sister. "Have we done something about crowd control? I don't think we want to go out and be mobbed tonight."

She nodded. "It's all taken care of. We're going to drive over in the van, then we'll slip in a side door and take the elevator up to the restaurant. The maitre d' promised to give us a table in a private area, so everything should be okay."

"Good." RC sent a relaxed smile around the room. "Okay, gang, welcome home. Do whatever you'd like, but you heard the lady of the house—be ready to go by 6 p.m. Tonight we're celebrating."

2

Though YB2's arrival caused a brief flurry among some of the younger kitchen staff, the maitre d' managed to get the band seated at a table next to the revolving restaurant's floor-to-ceiling windows. Noah sat next to Paige, and as the sunset splashed the western horizon with brilliant red and orange streaks, he found himself feeling sorry for her in a way he never had before.

She never asked for pity, and she hardly ever asked for help. RC's daughter was fiercely independent and proud of all she had learned to do on her own, but still . . . while everyone else oohed and ahhed over the incredible sights outside the window, she sat quietly at the table and sipped her water.

"Man, Paige, I wish you could see this," Noah whispered as the horizon shifted slowly with the turning of the restaurant. "The sky looks like it's on fire, and you

Noah

can see the lights of the city beginning to appear. Looks sort of like sparkling pepper on a dark tablecloth."

Paige's mouth softened as he struggled to explain, and a moment later she reached out to pat his hand. "Thanks, Noah."

The sun had set by the time the waiter brought their menus; the lights of Orlando completely spangled the darkness by the time their salads arrived. Noah sighed in gratitude when the conversation shifted from the awesome view to a recap of their last two weeks on the road. Aunt Rhonda wanted to hear all the funny stories about their encounters with fans at hotels, grocery stores, and rest stops, and it didn't take much to amuse her.

At the end of the meal, Josiah was in the middle of telling his story about the time his shoe caught on the hem of his pants and he tripped onstage, when the maitre d' approached their table. When Josiah abruptly stopped talking, the man bowed his head and leaned closer to RC. "I'm so sorry," he said, lacing his hands behind his back, "but apparently word of your presence has leaked. Security has informed me that the hotel lobby is filled with your fans—and more are gathering by the minute."

RC looked at Aunt Rhonda, then asked the maitre d', "Are the elevators the only way down?"

Rhonda frowned. "Any other time we'd be happy to sign autographs on our way out, but the kids are tired and we've promised them a weekend off."

The maitre d' inclined his head. "We do have the service elevators. They'll take you down to the employees' entrance that leads to the alley, then to the parking lot."

"We'll still have to walk through the parking lot to get to the van," Aunt Rhonda pointed out. "If people are driving in while we're going out, someone's bound to see us. And the last thing we want is a high-speed chase on the highway."

"I'll get the van and bring it to the alley." RC spoke in a light voice, but Noah was pretty sure RC was wishing they could be teleported from one location to another. He had often pointed out the danger of being spotted in a parking lot—if fans saw and gave chase, everyone ran the risk of getting into dangerous driving situations on busy streets.

Aunt Rhonda set her napkin on the table. "I'll get the van, Ron. No one knows who I am."

"I could go," Taz volunteered.

"Both of you sit still." RC thumped the table for emphasis. "None of the fans know me, and I'll be back in a minute. You two do enough for us; it's time I did something for you."

RC stood and left the table.

"What a guy," Aunt Rhonda said, lifting her iced-tea glass. "A good role model."

"You're a good role model too." Shane grinned at his aunt. "Aren't you paying the bill?"

A dimple appeared in Rhonda's cheek as she smiled. "Smart aleck. I ought to make you pay."

"Can't." Shane held up his empty hands. "I left my wallet at home."

"I've heard that excuse before . . . on my last five dates, I think."

Noah grinned at Aunt Rhonda as she fished her wallet from her purse. The woman was something else—he wasn't sure how old she was, but she was at least the age of his mother and the only woman he knew bold enough to wear a tattoo of a shoe on her shoulder for everybody to see. She had never married, devoting herself instead to RC and his children, and now she handled all the booking for YB2.

When the check had been paid, Aunt Rhonda looked around the table. "Everyone ready to go? Looks like Operation Mobilization is now underway." She stood, then hesitated as she slipped her purse onto her shoulder. "Paige, honey, why don't you take my hand? We might be in for some tricky footing."

Noah glanced beside him. Paige didn't argue, but he didn't think she wanted to be led through the kitchen holding her aunt's hand.

"I'll help her." He picked up Paige's hand and looped it through his arm. "There—just hang on to me, baby, and you'll be fine."

Paige laughed. "Promise you're not going to run me into a chair or something?"

"Nah. I couldn't be that uncoordinated if I tried. If I can ride the waves, I'm pretty sure I can slide both of us right on through a kitchen."

Noah grinned as the group followed the maitre d' through the huge kitchen. Several of the chef's helpers stood aside to let them pass, and two or three held slips of paper and pens. Noah was pretty sure they wanted autographs, but no one dared ask while the maitre d' was in the room.

They found the service elevator at the back of the kitchen, but a waiter had just entered it with a serving cart carrying food for a room service order in the hotel below. "I will take the cart off," the maitre d' said. He stepped forward and gestured to the waiter inside.

"Don't worry, you don't have to do that for us." Aunt Rhonda laid a firm hand on his arm. "We don't want anyone's dinner to get cold." She looked around the group. "Paige, you and Joe and I will go down on this ride, then—"

"I can wait." Paige lifted her head in the stubborn gesture Noah had come to recognize. He knew she didn't want special attention if she didn't need it, and Noah could tell Paige sometimes resented the way Aunt Rhonda hovered.

Aunt Rhonda shrugged. "Okay, then. Anybody who wants to go in the first shift, follow me."

Josiah, Shane, Taz, and Liane followed her into the elevator. One more person could have fit, but Noah caught Aunt Rhonda's eye and understood the meaning in her quirked brow: *Will you stay with Paige?*

"I'll wait here for the next trip," he announced,

slipping his hands into his pockets as he stepped away from the door. "See you guys in a few minutes."

Aunt Rhonda smiled her thanks as the elevator door closed.

"Thanks for waiting," Paige said as the elevator creaked away. "I appreciate it."

"Aw, that ride was too crowded," Noah answered, feeling good about waiting. RC had demonstrated that he could be a gentleman, and in his own small way, Noah had found a way to do the same thing.

Some days it felt cool to be a man.

3

Paige linked her hands around the top of her cane as she and Noah waited for the elevator. The scents of roasting meat and fresh bread filled her nose, while her ears rang with the sounds of running water, the elevator's hiss, clanging pots, and lowered voices giving orders. The kitchen workers seemed to be aware of their presence; they had been much louder when the group had first come into the kitchen.

"Hey—" she lifted her head toward Noah—"I think they're still watching us. Do you see any of them?"

She heard the quiet squeak of his shoes on the hard floor as he moved to look behind them. "Just a couple of people," he whispered, moving close enough that his shirt sleeve brushed her bare arm. "The main guy is a few feet away, but there's a girl kinda hovering behind a rack of dinner rolls."

Noah

Paige nodded. "Well, we might as well do something while we're standing here. Wanna ask the maitre d' if we can give out a few autographs?"

She smiled as Noah turned and called his offer to the maitre d'. Sure enough, within a moment someone had pressed a small notebook into Paige's hand—she felt the binder's curly spine and the length of a pen in her hand.

"Hey, Noah!" Not sure where he'd gone, she lifted the notebook in midair and asked, "Can I use your back?"

She heard Noah's laugh, then the sound of his shuffling through the small crowd that had gathered. When he stood firmly in front of her—she recognized him by his cologne—she braced the notebook on his back and signed her name.

"Hey—how do I know you're not writing on my shirt?" he joked. She heard his hair brush his collar as he turned his head.

"If I were writing on your shirt—" she lifted the notebook and held it out—"you'd feel it."

She signed three more slips of paper, then heard a series of murmured thank-yous followed by the ding of the elevator.

"Our ride's here." Noah turned and took her arm. "And it's empty this time. Mademoiselle, your coach awaits."

Following Noah, Paige moved into the elevator, then allowed the tip of her cane to touch the back wall. She turned around, facing front, then reached up to push her dark glasses more securely onto the bridge of her nose. "Thank you," she called to the people she sensed were watching from the kitchen. "We had a great dinner."

Noah laughed softly as he slapped at a button; then she heard the elevator doors close. After an instant of hesitation, the box began to move downward.

Paige lifted her head. She wasn't sure where Noah had settled in the elevator car; she could barely hear the soft sound of his shoes over the creaking machinery. "So, Noah . . . what'd you have for dinner?"

"I had the roast beef, and it was pretty good. Not like my mom makes it, though. Why—what'd you have?"

"Um . . . a hamburger." She frowned. Had the elevator been this loud when the others went down? The creaking noise seemed to be getting louder, and that smell—

She crinkled her nose. "Noah, do you smell that? Like something's burning—maybe burning rubber."

The words had no sooner left her lips when the elevator shuddered, then jolted and came to a halt. Paige stepped back and hit the wall on the bounce, then froze, one hand flattened against the wall.

"Man." Noah's voice squeaked. "What was that about?"

Paige sniffed again: the burning scent was still strong. "Noah, do you have any idea where we are?"

"We're in the elevator."

"I know that! I mean, can you tell what floor we're on?"

"Uh . . . somewhere between the thirty-eighth and

thirty-sixth, I think. The little lights on the numbers panel went out."

"No power?" She lifted her head. "Are the lights still on? Are we in the dark?"

"There's a light . . . an emergency light."

"That'd be a battery backup." Her mind flew over a list of tips Aunt Rhonda had taught her about how to handle emergencies, but none of those things seemed helpful now. She clutched at her shirt as another idea struck. "We need a phone! Do you have your cell phone?"

Noah groaned. "I left it back at the house. I didn't think I'd need it going out to dinner. You know how Aunt Rhonda hates it when our phones go off when we're eating."

"I think mine's in my purse." She reached for the bag hanging from her shoulder, then raked her hands through it, feeling pens, a compact, a tube of lipstick, a tin of Altoids . . . but no phone.

"Hey." Noah's voice had warmed. "There's a phone here in the wall. So there's no reason to panic, we'll just call for help."

No reason to panic? When they were hanging by a thread in an elevator that stunk of burning rubber and hung thirty-six, maybe thirty-seven, floors above a concrete abyss?

She heard a squeak of metal.

"Hello?" Noah said. "Hello? Anybody out there?"

Plastic slammed against a hard surface. "Noah, don't *break* it!"

"They won't answer." A thread of panic lined Noah's voice. "I don't think the phone is even hooked up. There's no dial tone or anything."

"Then we need to relax and be still." Paige drew a deep breath, grateful that she could feel the wall secure behind her back. "We don't need to move around a lot. If this thing is hanging by a thread—"

"It's not hanging by a thread. It's hanging by a wire, a heavy-duty cable."

"Cables . . . can fray, can't they?" Paige swallowed the boulder that had suddenly risen in her throat. Her mind filled with the vision of a multistranded cable breaking, wire by wire by wire . . . "Ohmigoodness. I don't want to die today. I'm ready to go to heaven, but I didn't get to tell Dad good-bye—"

"We're not going to die, Paige." Noah's voice was calm, almost too calm. He had to be in denial; he didn't seem to have a clue how dangerous a position they were in. "Liane told me all about this last year—she was reading a book on how to survive worst-case scenarios, you know, and one of the scenarios was being trapped in a falling elevator. What we're supposed to do is lie on the floor, facedown, with our hands over our heads—"

"You want me to lie on the *floor?*" Paige shrieked the words. "What in the world . . . that's crazy! That's like standing before a rushing car and saying, 'Okay, here I am! Hit me!'"

"Oh yeah?" Now she could hear exasperation in his tone. "Well, then—what would *you* do?"

Noah

"I think . . ." She bit her lip as she searched for an answer. "I think we should stand as still as possible. And if it falls, we should let it fall. But right before it hits the bottom, we'll hold hands and jump. Then we won't be on the ground when it hits, so we won't feel any impact at all."

"We won't know where the bottom is, Paige. The odds that we could jump at exactly the right instant are, like, a zillion to one. Plus, the rest of the elevator would fold in like a tin can. If we were standing up, we'd be crushed."

"Oh." Unable to answer, Paige slid down the back wall, taking care not to make any sudden moves.

"In a few minutes, RC will miss us," Noah said, sounding braver by the minute. "He'll send Taz or somebody to look for us, and they'll try to call the elevator."

"Oh, no!" Paige felt a moment of empty-bellied horror, the same feeling she always got at the top of a roller coaster. She covered her head with her hands. "We could hang here all day, but if someone calls the elevator, it's going to try to answer. That's when we'll fall."

"An elevator isn't a dog, Paige." Noah sounded as if he might be laughing at her. "It doesn't come when you whistle for it. In a few minutes, someone's gonna notice that it's not running—some bellman on the ground floor or one of those waiters with a room-service cart—and they'll call to see what's going on. You can be sure the hotel management will try to get it fixed as soon as possible. They won't want room service's dirty dishes in the regular elevators."

Paige nodded. Noah sounded so calm, so logical . . . and so completely unlike himself. Why wasn't he making jokes? Probably because beneath his bravado, he was as scared as she was.

A loud grating sound ripped through the air, sending a chill up her spine. "That's probably someone below us opening a door," Noah said. "They'll be trying to reach us soon."

She didn't say anything for a long moment, but counted the frantic beats of her heart. "Noah," she finally whispered, "I'm scared."

"I'm not exactly feeling confident myself."

"What should we do?"

"Well . . . I guess we should do what Lee's book said. Then we'll wait."

"And pray." Paige uttered the words as she stretched out on the floor. "God, *please* help us get out of here alive."

"He will. I have the feeling he's not finished with us yet."

"How do you know? Our last concert might have been our last concert."

"Scoot over, Paige—I think you're supposed to lie in the center of the elevator."

"I can't see where the center is, doofus."

"Slide about a foot to your left—there, that's good. Now I'm going to lie down next to you, and we'll pray together."

"Okay."

She heard the tiny *click* of shirt buttons hitting the floor as Noah stretched out next to her. Dust tickled her nose as she covered the back of her head with her hands.

"Lord, please send an elevator dude—someone who knows what they're doing," Noah prayed.

"Amen," she whispered. "And help Dad and the others realize we're missing."

Noah's voice shifted closer to her ear. "I'm sure they know we're missing."

"How do you know? They might have figured we stopped for autographs."

"They'll know better, Paige. We knew they were in a hurry to get away from the crowd downstairs. And Aunt Rhonda made it clear this wasn't a good night to sign autographs."

"Aunt Rhonda knows you love the crowds. She probably thinks you're off in a corner surrounded by screaming girls."

"Oh, she does not."

"Does too."

He let out a sigh of pure exasperation. "You're not helping matters."

"Well . . . you're not exactly helping, either." She smiled as she realized that Noah's crazy talk *was* helping a lot. He kept jabbing back at her, saying goofy things just to keep her from panicking.

"Hey," she said. "I'm sorry I called you a doofus."

"That's okay—I am a doofus sometimes."

"You're not. You pretend to be a clown, but I know you can be serious. I can hear it in your voice."

"Well . . . thanks. But if you saw my comedy act, you'd know I'm a no-talent clown."

"Somehow I doubt that."

Having run out of words, Paige lay on the floor in a quiet so thick that the only sound was the heavy rush of her breathing.

"I'm going to sneeze," she announced. "I'm allergic to dust, and it feels like there are two inches of it on this floor."

"So go ahead and sneeze."

"But if I do—what if it jars the car? We might fall."

"Your sneezes are that powerful?"

"Yep—they're Godzilla sneezes."

"So put your finger under your nose. That always stops my sneezes."

"How can I put my finger under my nose? You tell me to do all this stuff, but I can't put my finger under my nose if I've got my hands behind my head."

"We're going to be fine, Paige. These elevators have all kinds of safety mechanisms."

"The *nice* elevators have safety mechanisms. This is the employee elevator—does it look nice to you?"

"How would you know how it looks?"

Paige heard the sound of Noah's movement, then his head thunked against the floor. "It looks fine. There's even a certificate on the wall that says it passed inspection."

"Oh yeah? When?"

"A year ago."

"Great. A lot can happen in a year."

"You got that right."

They fell silent again, then Paige heard the slick whisper of something moving through the air. "What's happening? I heard something."

"What'd it sound like? Moving cables?"

"How on earth am I supposed to know? I don't even know what an elevator looks like, let alone how cables work. But I hear this whirring sound, and some creaking."

"I'm sure the repair people are coming. But I've been thinking that we should hope that when we *do* get out—"

"—We get out alone." Following his thought, she giggled. "Hey—what if we get to the bottom and have to walk through a pack of reporters?"

"Or photographers?" Noah was laughing so hard the elevator trembled. "We're gonna look awful. The front of my shirt's filthy, and you've got this big dusty smudge on your forehead and nose and chin—"

Paige opened her mouth to answer, but the elevator grumbled to life. She heard a click, then a groan, followed by the stomach-dropping sensation of a free fall.

"Noah!" Forgetting to shield her head, she fumbled for his hand.

"I've got you, Paige!"

The elevator fell away, sending great currents of rushing air over the outside of it. Then they seemed to rest on a cushion that caught the car for a moment, then gently lowered it to a safe landing.

Paige lay on the floor, as tense as a guitar string, until she heard the mechanical sound of sliding doors.

"We're here—and it's okay." Noah spoke low in her ear. "Let me help you up."

She pushed herself off the floor, realized that she had lost her glasses, and fumbled for them in a momentary panic until she felt someone slip them into her hand.

"They were on the floor," Noah said, helping her slide them on. "And there's a small crowd in the hall, but smile, keep your head up, and we'll be fine. And Paige—"

"Yeah?"

"Thanks for the adventure."

With no option but to trust him, Paige let him help her to her feet, then she lifted her head and followed him out. Her dad's voice was the first she recognized, followed by Aunt Rhonda's. Then a host of other voices crowded her ears: "Miss Clawson! Are you okay? Were you frightened? What happened? What were you thinking?"

"I'm so sorry," a man kept mumbling behind her. "So sorry. That car has been having difficulties, but we've never had this kind of trouble. You were never in any real danger because of the backup systems, but we're terribly sorry, so sorry . . ."

Pasting a smile onto her trembling lips, Paige held on to Noah's arm and let him lead her through the fray.

4

Sunday, October 3

Noah was dreaming of dancing with Paige in a foggy elevator when someone tapped his shoulder. He opened his eyes, half-expecting to see some dude wanting to cut in like a tuxedoed character in an old Fred Astaire movie, but when his eyes focused he saw only Aunt Rhonda. She was sitting in a lawn chair next to him, her broad sun hat on her head and a concerned look on her face.

"Sorry to wake you, Noah."

"It's okay." He cleared his throat and sat up. "I didn't mean to go to sleep, but that sun . . ."

"I know, it'll make you drowsy. It'll also burn you to a crisp." She gave him a mother-hen look. "Did you put on sunscreen?"

"Yes, ma'am. SPF fifteen."

Noah felt his nerves tighten when she looked at a pink slip in her hand and hesitated. "Listen, Noah,

a message came this morning while we were at church.
I just took it off the machine, so it's a few hours old . . .
but I thought you might want to answer it now. Or not."

Noah took the pink message slip from her hand.
Under "caller" she had written "Bill Dudash." Under
"message" she had scrawled "Your father would like to
see you when YB2 performs in Las Vegas later this month.
Call him if you're willing to get him tickets."

A long-distance number followed the message, and
at the sight of it Noah felt his mouth go dry.

He hadn't heard from his father in almost six years.
One day Bill Dudash had packed a suitcase and walked
out the door, leaving his family in California while he
began a new life in Las Vegas. Aside from the presents
that arrived for Noah every Christmas (which were never
opened), Bill Dudash seemed to have forgotten he even
had a son . . . until now.

Noah looked up to find Aunt Rhonda studying him.
"You want me to call him back, Noah?" she asked, her
tone gentle. "I could call him for you. The tickets are
no problem. I can have some set aside—"

"No—that's okay. I'll call him . . . as soon as I figure
out what I want to say."

She nodded, then pressed her hands to her tanned
knees and stood up. He'd never told her the entire story
of his parents' divorce, but Aunt Rhonda seemed to pick
up a lot through intuition.

He might talk to her later . . . but right now he
needed to think.

He looked up at the wide blue sky, where the wind pushed at scribbles of clouds. Funny, really, that his dad would call now. Last month Noah had been thinking a lot about his father because of the letter he'd received from his mom saying that his dog had died. Noah had had a hard time getting over that terrible news—partly because Justus had been his best friend and partly because the dog had been a present from his dad—the last thing he gave Noah before taking off.

Liane had suggested that writing a song about Justus might help Noah feel better, so nearly everyone in the group had helped him struggle to come up with lyrics and a tune. Paige had been the most helpful, and even Josiah had tried to teach Noah how to rhyme a line or two.

After a lot of erasing and starting over, he had finished the song and sung it for the group. Then when Noah had locked away the music in his guitar case, he'd figured he was over his feelings about Justus and his dad.

But now this—a phone call, coming from out of nowhere and for no reason. His dad had said he wanted to come to the YB2 concert, but why? It was a little late for Bill Dudash to start being a father.

Noah stared at the pool, pushing down a surge of anger that roared in his ears. He wanted to ignore this message the same way *he'd* been ignored for the last five years. Sure, his dad could come to the concert if he wanted to, but he could buy his sixty-five-dollar ticket with everyone else and stand in line for three hours with hordes of screaming girls. Why should he be granted any special favors? He hadn't cared one single bit about Noah when he destroyed their family . . . so why should Noah care about him now?

Noah jerked his head, pulling away from the memory as tears of rage rose in his eyes. RC was always saying that the first instinct is usually the wrong one, what the human half wants to do. But Noah's so-called spiritual half wasn't rising to this challenge. As a matter of fact, his inner "spiritual man" seemed to be napping.

So . . . maybe Bill Dudash should be ignored completely. If the inner spiritual guy voiced no objections, neither did Noah.

He wadded the paper in his palm, compressed it into the tiniest paper ball he could, then rolled it between his thumb and finger. He could flick it into the pool, where the water would soften and shred it in a matter of hours. He ought to do it—he had every right to.

But something wouldn't let Noah do it.

Maybe that little spiritual man wasn't asleep after all.

Just to be safe, Noah slipped the little pink ball into his shirt pocket, then went into the house for something cold to drink.

5

"Ouch!" Paige stumbled over something in the hall, then reached out to rub her bare toe. She knew almost every inch of their Florida home by memory, but living with six other people, three of whom were teenage boys, toes were likely to encounter stray tennis shoes, basketballs, and video games on the floor.

Kneeling on the carpet, she reached out to feel for whatever she'd kicked on her journey to the kitchen. There! The object was rubbery and round . . . and fuzzy. A tennis ball. The only tennis players were Shane Clawson and Lew Hargrave, one of the vice presidents for their label, Melisma Records. Lew wasn't in town today, which meant that Shane had to be the one who'd left this ball for her to trip over. She took a deep breath, about to yell out his name, then decided a softer approach might be more effective.

Noah

She stood, reached out to touch the wall, then took a few more steps toward the kitchen. She slowed when she heard the sound of Liane's and Noah's voices. They were speaking in hushed voices, and the sound of their private conversation sparked Paige's irritation.

Good grief, what was *wrong* with her? She wasn't usually this touchy. Shane always had the power to irritate her, but he was her brother, and brothers and sisters were expected to get on each other's nerves. But Liane and Noah were her friends; she could tell either of them anything, and they could confide in her—

But they were confiding in each other at the moment, and she had the distinct feeling that if she turned the corner they'd stop talking altogether.

She leaned against the wall and tilted her head toward the back of the house, a position that allowed her to listen closely. Since she had never had the sense of sight, she had sharpened her senses of smell and hearing to tell her what her eyes could not. She didn't hear a sound in the carpeted hallway, nor did she smell cologne or the sweat-drenched skin of any of the others.

Satisfied that no one else was near, she directed her full attention to the conversation.

"I don't know what to do," Noah was saying, his voice low and tight. "Part of me wants to tell him to buzz off and leave me alone, but another part knows that wouldn't be right. And you know what? I think I'm curious. I mean, I can barely remember what the guy even looks like. It might be nice to know."

"He's probably curious about you, too," Liane answered. She sighed heavily. "You never know, though—he could be looking for a handout. Maybe he thinks you're rich and famous and now you can give him money or something."

Noah snorted. "Fat chance. As if I'd do anything nice for him after what he did to me and my mom."

Liane didn't answer, and Paige lowered her head as the subject of the conversation became clear. Before last month when Noah talked about his family, he meant his mom and his dog, but last month the dog had died. For a long time Paige had assumed Noah's dad was dead, too, but then she learned he had walked out and left Noah and his mom years ago.

Paige understood. Her mom had done the same thing when she was only a few months old, but at least she hadn't totally disappeared. Paige and Shane used to spend their summers at their mother's home in Atlanta, but because it was hard for Paige to get around in a strange house, that plan had been scrapped. After YB2 began, Paige and Shane needed to work on music during the summer breaks, so now, for one week at Christmastime each year, their mom came to Florida and lived in the guesthouse, playing the role of polite visitor as the Clawsons opened their home to her.

It wasn't a great situation, but Paige had learned to deal with it. Aunt Rhonda had become like a mom, and her dad was always around when she needed him. Her mother was more like an aunt—someone to be kind and respectful to, especially at Christmas.

Families were a strange thing. You had no say about the people God put in your family, and most of the time you couldn't do a thing to control their behavior. Families were supposed to love and support each other, but happiness wasn't guaranteed . . . and even though most people figured out a way to make things work, everyone was bound to get hurt at times.

Someone had obviously hurt Noah, and now he didn't know what to do about it.

"I think," Liane said, her voice slow and thoughtful, "that you should call your dad. Yeah, he was awful to you and your mom, but treating him the same way isn't going to make things better. Call him and tell him you'll leave two tickets for him at the will-call window. You don't have to give him a backstage pass if you don't want to see him, but at least you'll have done more for him than he did for you."

"Maybe."

"I know it's probably the last thing you want to do, but you'll feel awful if you blow him off," Liane added.

Noah snorted a laugh. "'Forgive and forget,' right? You think I should just let it go and pretend it's no big deal that he up and took off?"

"No . . ." Liane said carefully. "I think you should do what's right."

Noah sighed heavily. "You're right, I know you are. My head tells me one thing, but my gut tells me something else. I want to go up to him and pound him into the ground, I really do."

Liane laughed. "Don't listen to your gut, Noah. Listen to your head and your heart. Go into the office and call him. Then you can put this out of your mind for a while, at least until we get to Las Vegas. Then you can decide whether or not you want to let him come backstage."

A moment of silence filled the kitchen, then Noah chuckled softly. "Thanks, Lee. I don't know what I'd do without you to talk to."

The sound of a bar stool scraping across the floor shot through Paige like a bullet. Startled, she ducked her head and hurried down the hall toward the bedrooms. She would *die* if one of them came around the corner and caught her eavesdropping.

When it was clear no one had followed her, she reached out for the staircase banister, then sank to the bottom step and propped her elbows on her knees. Resting her chin in her palms, she sighed.

RC didn't allow YB2 members to date, but Noah and Liane were obviously close. And why shouldn't they be? They weren't brother and sister like she and Shane were, and Noah looked up to Liane because she was smart. Whenever anybody had a problem, they went to Liane first because she either knew the answer or knew where to find it.

And Liane was pretty—she had to be. Paige had no idea what "pretty" looked like, but she could tell that people thought Liane fit the word. Her long, silky hair swished over her back when she moved, and she had a way of laughing that made others laugh with her even if her logic was beyond them.

So . . . Noah must love Liane. How could he help it? Even though they couldn't date, someday they'd probably come off the road and go to the same college. After Noah graduated as a professional surfer and Liane got degrees in medicine, law, and astronomy, those two would move to some exotic place and get married . . .

And in all the years to come, Noah would never think of Paige in the same way he thought of Liane. For one thing, she was blind, which meant she was practically invisible. Once people learned that dull, lifeless eyes lived behind her dark glasses, they tended to clear their throats, excuse themselves, and walk away, preferring to talk with anyone else about anything.

Most people didn't know how to talk to a blind person. Other people actually *shouted* at her, as if she couldn't hear, either. She'd had people offer her wheelchairs at amusement parks and the handicapped stalls in restrooms, as if blindness required an extra wide door and a low sink. And lots of times when she traveled with someone else— it didn't matter who—people spoke through the other person, as if she needed an interpreter.

Her blindness often struck people with momentary cases of pure stupidity, but Noah had never treated Paige in any weird way. He'd been a little curious when they first met, as most people were, but within hours he had seemed to accept her like any other girl. After a few days, when he had learned that Paige wrote most of the group's songs with Shane and RC, he'd begun to treat her with extra respect.

In the elevator at the restaurant, when they'd been inches away from death, he'd talked to her as a friend— a close friend. That had been the single most intense and personal conversation she'd ever had with any- body, and now, to hear him talking about something personal and intense with Liane . . .

She groaned as the truth hit her smack between the eyes. She was *jealous*. Before today she would not have believed that she could ever be jealous of anyone in YB2—they were all too close, more like brothers and sisters than friends. But there was no denying the ugly little nettle that had burrowed into her heart—it scratched every time she thought about Noah and stung every time she heard Liane's voice.

Jealousy was such an ugly thing. But she couldn't deny that it was alive and real and eating away at her heart.

"Why, Paige!"

Paige flinched as Aunt Rhonda's voice fell upon her ear. She should have heard her aunt's footsteps on the stairs, but she'd been too focused on her problem.

"Yeah?"

"What are you doing on the stairs—and what's this on your cheek? You're crying?"

Sniffing, Paige swiped the wetness away. "Am I? Sorry, didn't realize."

"Aw, hon." Aunt Rhonda settled into the space

between Paige and the banister. "You want to talk about it?"

Paige lifted her head. "Are we alone?"

A smile lined Aunt Rhonda's voice. "We are indeed. RC and the guys are throwing a Frisbee out back, and Liane's reading by the pool."

Paige swallowed as her throat tightened with emotion. She couldn't explain everything pressing on her heart—it was too ugly to admit, even to Aunt Rhonda—but she could ask a question or two that had been bothering her.

"Aunt Rhonda," she said, turning her head toward the woman, "what is beautiful?"

"You mean . . . like the dictionary definition?"

"No—*your* definition."

"Ah." Rhonda's voice took on a thoughtful tone. "Beauty is . . . well, there are many kinds of beauty. In art, beautiful things are often symmetrical, like a clean room in soft colors with matching pillars on each side. A human face is beautiful when the eyes match, the lips curve exactly the same on both sides, the nose is evenly proportioned. Then again, beauty can be the unexpected—a splash of color in a black-and-white landscape, a crystal glittering out from within a chunk of rock, a beauty mark on delicate pale skin. Beauty is subjective, honey—it's different things to different people." Her voice gentled. "Why do you ask?"

Paige shrugged. "I was just wondering . . . if I'll ever be beautiful."

"Oh, honey." Rhonda's arm slipped around Paige's shoulder and drew her close. "Don't you know how beautiful you are? When you're onstage playing your piano, the spotlight hits your brown hair in such a way—well, you look like an angel. You're beautiful, everyone thinks so. Your dad and I certainly do."

"But . . . do the boys?"

Aunt Rhonda drew in her breath. "You mean our boys?" She laughed. "Well, brothers rarely think of their sisters as beauty queens, so Shane would probably say you're cute, not beautiful. I'm sure the other guys would say you're cute, too."

Paige bit her lip. "Even with my glasses off?"

A moment of silence followed, in which Paige could tell her aunt was fumbling for words. "When your glasses are off, honey, we see your eyes—"

Paige threw up her hand. "You don't have to tell me how ugly they are. I can feel them, I know they aren't quite right."

Aunt Rhonda caught her hand. "Do you want me to be honest, sweetie?"

"Yes . . . I think so."

"Okay, then. Your eyes—well, you have to remember they've never been exercised like other people's. So your eyelids are sort of relaxed and half-closed most of the time. That's not ugly, it's different. But people don't always understand different. And sometimes they can be cruel with their comments."

Paige nodded. She understood cruelty—when she was

Noah

younger, she had gone to special classes at a school for the blind where she'd learned to read Braille and walk with her cane. Many times while she was waiting at the bus stop, her ears had picked up the taunts from mean kids on the street.

"Sweetie." Smelling of lilacs and soap, Aunt Rhonda drew Paige closer. "You have to understand that a woman has two kinds of beauty—inside and out. Your outside package can be perfect in every way, but if your beauty on the inside isn't intact, the outside loses a lot of its shine. On the other hand, a girl can look rather plain, but when her inner beauty fires up, she glows and no one can take their eyes off her."

Paige nestled into the soft space between her aunt's chin and shoulder. "How do you fire up the inner beauty?"

"By doing things you love to do . . . and being happy in the process. You set it ablaze when you are comfortable being you . . . and when you love the people in your life."

Aunt Rhonda laughed softly. "I remember an afternoon when I was about ten—I found myself thinking about the same things you're thinking about. I sat down in front of my bedroom mirror and saw a plain girl with wide eyes, buckteeth, and hair with a mind of its own. I knew right then that I would not be beautiful in the eyes of the world . . . but then I remembered the verse where Peter wrote that we shouldn't be concerned about outward beauty from fancy hairstyles, expensive jewelry, or beautiful clothes. He said we should be known for beauty inside that doesn't fade—a gentle and quiet spirit that's beautiful and precious to God."

Paige shifted. "Is that when you decided to get a tattoo?"

Rhonda pinched Paige's arm. "No, silly, that came later. No, that day as a ten-year-old I prayed that God would make me gentle and quiet and beautiful on the inside . . . because I knew that kind of beauty would leak out through my plain face. And you know what? I think God honored that prayer. Don't think that because I never married I never had the opportunity—I dated several nice men before I realized God had a different plan for me. I had a family waiting, but I wouldn't find it through a husband."

Paige lifted her head. "*We* were your family?"

She felt the gentle pressure of her aunt's arm. "Exactly right. When your mother left, I knew Ron would need help. You were only a baby and Shane was still in diapers. So I came here, and I've never regretted a minute of my life. I still date on occasion, and I don't think any of my guy friends would say I'm unattractive."

"I'm glad you came to live with us."

Rhonda pressed a kiss into Paige's hair. "So am I. Because I've been able to see how a skinny little baby girl has grown into a beautiful and confident young woman."

"Thanks, Aunt Ro." Paige slipped her arm around her aunt and squeezed.

"You're welcome, honey." Rhonda's hand stroked Paige's cheek. "Now wipe those tears and go outside with the others. You've worked hard and you deserve some time to relax. You don't need to be moping around the house."

Paige sniffed again, then stood and nodded. What would she do without her aunt?

6

Noah barged through the doorway of the room he shared with Josiah, then grinned at the sight of the younger boy spread-eagled on the floor.

"The game wore you out, did it?" he joked, stepping over Josiah on his way into the bathroom. "See what playing with the big boys can do?"

"I can hold my own," Josiah answered, panting. "But I didn't expect you and Taz to double-team me."

Noah laughed as he ran cold water in the sink. "We weren't double-teaming you, dude, we were trying to get away from RC. That man plays physical."

"Tell me about it."

"Besides, if you didn't want to play ball, you could have stayed in the pool with Shane."

"No, thanks. I'm gonna grow gills if I spend much more time in the water."

Noah splashed his face then pulled a towel from the hanger on the wall. When he stepped back into the room, he saw that Josiah had managed to pick himself up and drop onto his own bed.

A stretch on the old rack would feel good after a blistering game of hoops.

Noah sat on the edge of his bed, then looped the towel around his neck. Josiah's eyes were half-closed, so the kid could be either half-asleep or half-awake.

"Hey, Joe." He waited until one of the boy's eyelids lifted. "Can I ask you something?"

The eyelid closed again. "Yeah. Sure."

"Okay . . . are you tight with your dad?"

Both of Josiah's eyes flew open. "Huh?"

"I mean . . . do you play ball with your dad?"

"My dad's five feet four." Josiah rolled onto his side, then propped his head on his hand. "He's not much for basketball. But we do other stuff together."

"Like what?"

Josiah lifted one shoulder in a shrug. "Like . . . watch sports on TV. And go camping. My dad loves to camp and fish and stuff like that."

Noah sank back against the pillows on his bed. "Do you miss your dad when you're here?"

Josiah blinked. "Like . . . do I cry into my pillow every night?"

"No, man. Like . . . do you miss him at all?"

"Sure." Josiah pounded his pillow, then lay flat on his bed and looked up at the ceiling. "I mean, not all the time or anything, but there are times when I think my dad would really like to see something we're seeing, or do something we're doing."

Noah nodded. "Okay." He said nothing else, but picked up the basketball on his bed and twirled it between his index fingers.

Josiah leaned forward, his eyes serious. "Why do you want to know about my dad?"

"Just wondering."

When Josiah didn't move, Noah realized the boy wanted more of an answer. "Well—" he rested the ball on his chest—"I haven't seen my dad in years, see. So this morning Aunt Rhonda tells me that he called the office and left a message—he wants to hook up with me at our concert in Vegas. So now I don't know what to do. Part of me wants to tell him to go jump in a lake, and the other part of me . . . well, I guess I want to see him. I'm kinda curious." He shot a look at his roommate. "Wouldn't you be?"

Josiah nodded. "Sure, I would. So . . . what are you going to do?"

Noah shrugged. "I dunno. At first I was angry because of what he did to us five years ago, then Liane said I should at least leave him two tickets at the will-call window. But I don't know."

Josiah seemed to study the pattern in the plaid comforter on his bed, then he grinned. "You don't have a brother or sister to ask, huh?"

Noah shook his head. "Naw."

"Well . . . you could always ask your mom. After all, she knows him better than you do."

Noah stared at the younger boy for a moment, then felt the corner of his mouth lift in a smile. Sometimes wisdom popped up in the most unlikely places.

"Thanks, dude." He tossed the basketball to Josiah, then stood and moved toward the door. "You're brilliant."

It really *was* a good idea, he realized as he strode toward the office. His father had left his mother to make all the decisions about his future, so why not let her decide whether he should see his dad again? She hadn't been at all pleased about Dad's desertion, so when he called to tell her what Dad asked, she was bound to be ticked.

And she'd happily make his decision about what to do.

Their free weekend vanished like dew under the hot morning sun. By the middle of the following week, Noah was beginning to feel like he'd been riding the endless broken line of asphalt all his life.

They were on their way to the convention center for their next concert, but RC had asked Larry to stop by the hotel to pick up a bundle of mail he was expecting from Aunt Rhonda. As Noah watched RC jog into the hotel, he realized he didn't even know what city they were in—he'd been totally out of it all day, thinking about his mom and dad. Though his mom was miles away now, he still felt her presence in his life. His dad was also miles away, but he felt nothing but an aching emptiness whenever he thought about his father.

"Noah?" RC stepped onto the bus with a box of mail under his arm, then pulled out an official-looking blue envelope and tossed it to Noah. "Express package for you. I think you should open it right away; it might be important."

Surprised, Noah studied the return address. The package was from his mom—he'd spoken to her on Sunday night. As he'd suspected, she had been upset about his dad having the gall to ask if he could meet Noah in Las Vegas, but she hadn't mentioned anything so urgent she'd have to send an express mail package.

Noah ripped open the envelope, then withdrew a letter and a plain manila envelope.

Hastily, he scanned the handwritten pages:

Dear Noah,

After your call tonight, honey, I was gripped by second thoughts. You know, I was angry and crushed when your father left us, but that happened so long ago, and I've made peace with that hurt part of myself. The Lord has been good to us; he has comforted us and brought us through the pain, so why should we cling to it? And while I was sitting there, praying about these things, I realized I had led you astray. I told you to ignore your Dad—now I'm telling you that you're going to have to make your own decision.

I know it'd be easier if I made it for you, but you're a young man, and part of growing up is learning to make the right choices. I'll give you advice—when you need it—but ultimately, you're going to have to choose your own paths.

So I've sent you a few pictures—some little moments of your life you may have forgotten. When we've been hurt, it's easy to forget the good times and cherish our wounds instead, but we'll never heal if we keep doing that.

Sweetheart, I love you. You're a great guy. And I honestly believe your father loves you, too. How could he not?

His request for tickets may be his way of trying to move past his own pride and embarrassment to reach out to you. Pray about it and do what you feel led to do, but now I'm thinking you should call him. Talk to him. And invite him to your concert.

But before you decide, take a look at these photographs, and study the man you see in the pictures. He was a good man when I fell in love with him. I want to believe he is a good man still . . . and I know even good men make mistakes.

Call me if you want to talk.

Love,
Mom

Ignoring the warbling of Josiah's handheld video game from behind him, Noah poured the contents of the manila envelope onto the empty seat to his right. His mom had pulled at least two dozen photographs from the family albums—he saw pictures of himself on a tricycle with his dad stooped and running behind him, photos of a blond kid pedaling a little bike with training wheels as his dad hovered near, holding him upright. There was a shot of Noah sitting behind a birthday cake with one candle stuck in the center—his dad sat behind him, his eyes intent on Noah and his mouth puckered, as if he were trying to teach his son how to blow it out.

Noah scooped up a handful of the pictures to study them more closely. One showed his mom and dad, their arms linked around each other, both smiling for the camera. Who had taken this shot, and when? They both looked so young, so happy.

He blinked as his eyes unexpectedly filled with tears, and when RC stood from the front seat and turned to face the back of the bus, Noah lowered his head so RC wouldn't see the emotion on his face.

RC walked to the seat where Shane was studying and rested his hand on his son's shoulder. Shane asked something about an algebra problem, and RC replied in a low tone. Noah watched them—if his dad were still living at home, would he help Noah with his homework? Or would he be one of those never-around dads who worked all the time to support the family? Silly question, really— he'd never know.

RC straightened and moved to check on Paige, who sat behind Shane, and in that moment Noah knew RC would stop at his seat next. They were back on the road, heading to the convention center to prepare for tonight's concert. In these quiet hours while the crew set up the

Noah

stage, RC often took time to visit with his team members. After all, he was responsible for their well-being while they were together . . . he was more like a father than Noah's dad had ever been—

No, that wasn't right. These pictures proved that once, years ago, Bill Dudash had been a big part of Noah's life.

Noah was stuffing the photos back into the envelope when RC sank onto the armrest across from Noah's seat. "Everything okay?" he asked, one brow lifting as he nodded toward the remains of the envelope.

Noah nodded. "Yeah. My mom sent me some stuff."

RC waited a moment, then slipped his hands into his pockets. When he spoke, he kept his voice low so it wouldn't carry through the entire bus. "I hope you don't think I'm trying to pry, Noah, but Rhonda told me about your father's call. She also told me you haven't called him back yet—at least, not to her knowledge."

Noah hung his head. "Yeah, that's right. I don't know what to do."

"Did you speak to your mother about it?"

"Yeah—and she told me to ignore him. But then she changed her mind." Noah held up the manila envelope. "She sent pictures to remember him by. She says it's my decision, but now she's thinking I need to invite him."

RC pushed his bottom lip forward in thought. "I think your mom's a wise woman."

Noah shrugged, not sure he wanted to agree. "Yeah . . . sometimes."

"She obviously understands the power of forgiveness."

Noah squinted at RC. "What's that got to do with anything?"

RC inclined his head as a small smile touched his lips. "I think your mom has taken big steps toward forgiving your father. She told you to ignore him at first because she was deeply hurt . . . but sending those pictures shows that she has learned to forgive your dad. She doesn't hate him."

Noah snorted. "Sometimes I think she ought to."

"That's what most people would think. But how do you think God wants you to treat your dad?"

Noah shrugged. "Forgive him, I guess. But I forgave my father a long time ago. We moved on and got over him."

"Really? Forgiveness is more than a word, Noah—it's an attitude. You can say you've forgiven someone, but if you're still harboring bad feelings, your forgiveness is only window dressing."

Noah crossed his arms and looked away. RC didn't know how it felt to have a dad walk out the door without a word of explanation. In the Orlando house Noah had seen pictures of RC and his father—RC's dad was an old man now, but he kept in close touch with RC, Rhonda, Shane, and Paige. He lived in an assisted living center on the outskirts of the city, and the Clawsons visited him whenever they could.

"Tell me this," RC said, looking at the ceiling. "When we become Christians, we ask Jesus to forgive our sins, right?"

Noah shrugged. This was kid stuff. "Sure."

"Okay." RC smiled. "So suppose I do something wrong—let's say I cheat one of our concert promoters and refuse to pay for the work he's done. If I feel sorry about that and ask the Lord to forgive me, will he?"

Noah suppressed a groan. Why was RC treating him like a child? "Yes, of course he will. Because . . . he's God. He always forgives us. That's his job."

RC snapped his fingers. "Exactly right. It's our job too, Noah. Whether we feel like it or not."

Noah took a wincing little breath as the reason for RC's questions became clear. He raked his hand through his hair. "But that's my point! God doesn't harbor bad feelings, but he's God! I'm just me, and my dad hurt my mom and me something terrible when he walked out."

"You don't think we've hurt God in the same way?"

Noah thought a moment. "No. Not in the same way."

"Haven't we walked out on him—as individuals, and as a human race? He loved us, he created us, and one by one, we chose to follow our own way rather than his."

Noah squinched his eyes shut. "This is too much, RC. I can't think about it now. I see what you're saying, but I can't be God. No way."

RC pressed his lips together for a moment, then nodded. "You'll figure it out, Son." He stood and clapped a hand on Noah's shoulder. "And when you do, I'm sure you'll do the right thing and pay the price."

"What price is that?"

"That's for you to decide. But forgiveness always costs

the forgiver something. The more you forgive, the more it'll cost you."

Noah said nothing as RC walked away. He sat in silence for a long moment, wishing he were as sure of himself as RC was.

8

From the seat in front of Noah, Paige nodded
her head, pretending to rock with the music while she
listened to the conversation between Noah and her dad.
She was wearing her headphones, but no one knew
the music had stopped so she could listen to what was
bothering Noah.

Now she understood more than she wanted to . . .
and she knew Noah needed help. He'd talked to Liane,
her dad, and his mom . . . so why wouldn't he talk to
her? When they were trapped in the elevator together,
she had thought—*hoped*—that he'd begun to see her as
someone other than RC's daughter and the blind girl.

She slipped her headphones from her ears, then
leaned forward and stuffed them into the pocket on the
seat back. Tilting her head, she listened for sounds of
anyone near—shoes scuffing against the floor, books

Noah

being tossed into the overhead luggage rack—and heard nothing.

Convinced she had a few minutes to talk, she stood and felt her way around the seat, then dropped into the empty space at Noah's side.

She'd startled him. He didn't gasp or say anything, but she felt his arm tense, a subtle flexing that seemed to show more curiosity than alarm.

"Well, hi," he said, a note of surprise now evident in his voice. "Were you aiming for this seat, or did you just happen to nearly fall into my lap?"

"I'm more coordinated than that." She took pains to keep her voice light. "I thought I might like to sit with you a while."

"Well . . . I'm honored." He was smiling now—she could hear it in his tone. "Wow. Two Clawsons in an hour. First your dad, now you. If Shane comes toward this seat, you'll have to tell him to leave, though. No room."

She suppressed a giggle. "Shane's studying. I can hear his brain cells sizzling from over here."

"You don't cut him much slack, do you?"

"You should hear some of the things he used to call me when we were little." Lightly, she reached out and patted his arm. "Don't take me too seriously, Noah."

"Okay."

"Like the other night in the elevator—I didn't really think we were going to die."

"Sure you didn't."

"I didn't."

"Coulda fooled me."

"Yeah, I was scared. But that's it." She shrugged slightly, then folded her hands in her lap. My goodness, how did girls talk to guys who weren't their brothers? She'd never had any trouble talking to Shane or Josiah or even Noah before . . . well, before she started thinking of him in a different way.

But she wasn't here to talk about her crazy feelings for him. YB2 had a rule about that—if you found yourself thinking about someone as more than a friend, you had to keep your feelings to yourself. RC didn't want dating in YB2, because those relationships could become distracting on the road full-time. And if the relationship ended, it could be painful and awkward for the whole group.

But once Aunt Rhonda had admitted that sometimes you couldn't help feeling the way you felt. Sometimes you just had to feel a certain way until you used the feeling up and didn't feel that way anymore. And right now she liked Noah—no, she *Liked* him—and because she *Liked* him, she wanted to do something to help him get over this trouble with his father. And while the others had filled his head with thoughts about whether he should call or not call and forgive or not forgive, she wanted to suggest something else—

"Noah." She turned to face him. "Remember the song you wrote?" The song Noah had written last month was about far more than his dog. It had been a song about his father, about pain and loss and where to find comfort. They had all heard the song and talked about how good it was; Shane had even suggested recording it. But then they'd gotten caught up in their busy schedule, and everyone seemed to have forgotten about Noah's song.

"Um . . . yeah. What about it?"

"We all thought it was really good, remember?"

"Everyone was just being nice. Nobody's said a word about it since."

"We got distracted, Noah—and besides, your version was only a rough cut. I think you should keep working on it."

Doubt filled his voice. "I'm no songwriter, Paige. I'm done with it."

"You're done with the lyrics and the melody. But you could still work on the arrangement or at least help me with it. And we could put a vocal chart together and play the finished version for my dad. If he likes it, he could get a track laid so we could perform it in the program."

This time she heard a gasp. "Perform it? Are you *nuts?*"

"It's a good song," she said, more quietly. "A song lots of kids will relate to. I think you should keep going with it."

She heard the swish of his hair as he shook his head. "Aw, man. I don't know anything about arranging an instrumental track."

"That's where I can help you. With my keyboard—" she pointed to the seat she'd just left—"we can fill in all the instrumental parts. I know you wrote it just for yourself, but you could really do something with it . . . and I'm hoping you will."

For a moment she heard nothing but the bleep, warble, and click-click-click of Josiah's video game, then Noah squeezed her hand. "You're sure about this?"

"Sure I'm sure."

"Okay, partner. We'll work on it. But if the song stinks or if RC hates it, we'll drop it, okay?"

She squeezed his fingers in reply. "Thanks, Noah. I appreciate this more than I can say."

Because I'm not allowed to tell you what I'm really feeling.

9

An hour after the bus pulled into the loading dock
at the civic center, Noah helped Taz unload the luggage
bays and found himself thinking about Paige's request.
So . . . she really liked his song. He'd been afraid she and
the others were only being nice when they complimented
him on it.

If they could work the song into an arrangement,
maybe perform it a few times to see how it went over
with the audience . . . who knows, maybe they'd record
it on an album. Maybe he'd see his name listed in the
album credits—he could even earn royalties! He'd share
them with Paige, of course, because he never could have
put the song together without her help.

He thought back to that frustrating time when he'd
struggled to come up with a title. He'd been so sad when
his dog died . . . and that grief tasted the same as the

Noah

unbelievable sadness he'd felt when his dad left home. So the song about Justus ended up being about his dad, too, and the only "happy ending" he could come up with was the same ending he tried in real life—he was trusting heaven to help him through the rough spots. When bad things happened, God didn't sweep down with a magic wand to make things right, but he did give his children strength to get through it.

Noah walked back to the loading dock, stepped into the sunshine, then went down the concrete stairs. Taz and Shane were on the pavement pulling costume bags and prop cases from the bus's luggage bays. Noah accepted a load of costume bags from Taz, then trudged back up the steps with YB2's soundman, his thoughts churning as he followed the paper signs to the dressing rooms.

"Hey, Noah," Taz said, dropping a trunk with the girls' costumes outside their dressing room door. He paused to stretch his muscular arms. "What's on your mind, man? You don't seem like yourself today."

Noah shrugged as he draped a long costume bag over the trunk. "Just thinking, I guess."

Taz slipped his hands into his pockets. "Care to share?"

Noah bit his lip, then jerked his head toward the hallway. "Going to get another load?"

"Yeah."

"Okay." They had walked only a few steps when Noah decided to let it all out. "My dad called to ask for tickets to the concert in Vegas. Trouble is, I haven't seen him in five years. Everybody else is telling me I need to forgive him, and RC said that means I'll have to pay a price—but I can't figure out what that price is supposed to be. I mean, can you put a dollar value on all the days and weeks and months I've been without a dad when I needed one?"

Taz shook his head. "Every kid needs a dad. It really stinks that yours left you alone."

"Yeah—I know I'm not perfect, but I wasn't the worst kid in the world, either. For a long time I thought I must have really messed up to make Dad leave, but Mom said I didn't do anything. She said every son deserves a loving father, but people don't always get what they deserve."

They walked in silence a moment more, then passed through the narrow security office by the loading dock. Noah nodded to the security guards who were watching the unloading with bored expressions, then he found himself wondering if either of these two guys had kids. If so, were they good fathers?

"Hey." The eyes of one of the guards widened in astonishment as he stared at Noah. "You're one of *them*. One of the singers."

Noah felt the corner of his mouth dip downward. "Yeah? So?"

"So you're out here hauling gear? I thought you guys would be sitting with your feet propped up somewhere."

Noah shook his head, then turned to follow Taz back down to the bus. "Somebody's got to bring in the stuff."

"Yeah, but not you guys. Wait a minute, will ya?" The guard turned to the desk, rifled through a stack of documents, then reached out with a pen and paper in his hand. "Can I get your autograph? It's for my kids. My son and daughter are big fans—they made me go out and get tickets the day they went on sale."

Smiling, Noah and Taz paused to autograph the man's blank page. And as he signed his name, Noah thought of his own dad, who could have ordered tickets for the YB2 concert when they went on sale. But his dad wanted *free* tickets, and he didn't deserve them.

What his father deserved was a ton of pain and grief. He certainly didn't deserve two free tickets to the Las Vegas concert.

When they had finished signing, Taz and Noah kept moving toward the loading dock, then trotted down the concrete steps.

"So?" Taz asked. "Figure out what you're going to do about your dad?"

"He doesn't deserve free tickets. I do know that."

Taz bit his lip, then nodded. "Maybe not. But we don't deserve everything we get, either. Do you and I really deserve to be here, in YB2? Yeah, we're pretty good at what we do, but do you honestly believe you're the best singer in America? I know I'm not the best sound guy."

Noah laughed as he led the way to the luggage bay, where Shane had lined up the last few cases on the pavement. "Coulda fooled me, Taz. I always thought you were the best."

Taz laughed. "Man, any guy with ears and a little technical know-how could handle my job. And good singers really aren't hard to find. But the truth is, RC prayed and we're the ones God sent his way. So we're blessed. But we sure don't deserve all the cool things that have happened to us."

Noah picked up the guys' costume bags and slung them over his shoulder, then reached down to lift another trunk. "So you're saying I don't really belong in YB2?"

"No, man." Taz's broad face split into a smile. "I'm just saying that God doesn't give us stuff or punish us based on how good we are. We don't deserve heaven, but he made a way for us to have it. And yeah, RC was right. God paid a pretty big price for it, too."

Without speaking, Noah walked with Taz into the guys' dressing room, then hung the bags in an empty locker. Taz muttered a "see ya later" and left the room, but Noah sank into a folding chair to think.

Jesus forgave, and he gave his life to pay that price. So if Noah were to forgive his dad—even *begin* to forgive him—then it would cost something.

Like . . . maybe this feeling that his dad deserved to miss the Las Vegas concert. If Noah could get past that, his dad could watch the performance, see Noah onstage, and realize all he'd abandoned.

Lifting his chin, Noah stood. He could call the box office at the MGM Grand Garden Arena in Las Vegas and reserve two tickets for his dad. The gesture wouldn't cost anything . . . except his pride.

And his anger.

But maybe he'd be better off without those things.

10

An hour later, Noah found RC with Taz at the soundboard in the center of the mammoth civic center.

"Um, RC—can I borrow your cell phone?"

"Sure." RC fished the official group phone from his pocket and tossed it to Noah. Unlike their personal cell phones, which group members carried only on days off, this phone was supposed to be used only for emergencies and phoning home. Noah was pretty sure this would be an approved call.

"Thanks."

He took the phone and walked about six rows down into the semidarkness, then slipped into one of the folding seats. Leaning forward, he pulled the wrinkled pink paper from his jeans pocket. The message slip had been manhandled in the last few days, but the number was still legible.

Noah

His heart pounded as he punched in the string of digits. What would he say if his dad answered? "Hi, this is Noah, your long-lost son"? Should he be a smart aleck or be serious?

He didn't need to decide. After two rings, an answering machine picked up: "Hello, we're not home. Leave your number and we'll call you back."

Noah hadn't heard his dad's voice in five years, but the voice in his ear sounded familiar. And who was this "we"? He must have gotten married again . . . or maybe he had a roommate.

Noah looked up at the domed ceiling as he spoke into the phone. "Hi . . . I'm looking for Bill Dudash. Dad, if this is the right number, I just wanted you to know I'm leaving two tickets for you at the will-call window for the Vegas concert—you know, at the MGM Grand. Hope you can make it."

He hurried to press the Off button before anyone could pick up. He didn't want to talk to anyone, didn't want to have to explain anything.

But there—he'd just done something right. He had repaid evil with good, turned the other cheek, all that Bible stuff. His mom and RC and Liane would be happy because he'd done the right thing. Now he could forget about his dad—if the man came to the concert, fine. If he didn't come—fine again. Noah had done his part.

Feeling more settled than he had in a long time, Noah stood and looked around for RC.

11

Sitting with Noah at the table in the center of the bus, Paige played a G chord on her piano. "Okay, Noah— sing your first verse for me, but go slow. I want to try some chords."

Nodding, Noah strummed his guitar and began to sing what he'd written last month:

> "I thought life would sorta flow by,
> I never had much reason to cry,
> Until you left me alone.
> I thought I'd caught the golden ring,
> Life offered me so many things,
> Until my heart turned to stone."

"Okay." Paige played a few more chords, hummed part of the melody again, then pointed to Noah. "Are you gonna write this down?"

Noah

"Yeah."

She heard the rustle of papers as she played a chord again. "Okay, we're starting in the key of G—why does it have to be that key?"

"'Cause it's one of the few I know on my guitar." Noah laughed, then lowered his voice to a more serious note. "Seriously—I just like it. It fits my voice."

Paige shrugged. "It's fine, I was only curious. Okay— we move from G to a C chord, then to a D-seven." She waited until she heard the tiny sounds of a pen pushing across paper. "That's pretty basic. I could spice it up a little . . . if you help by telling me what you like."

Actually, she could have spiced it up without his input, but one of the reasons she'd volunteered to help was because she wanted to spend more time with him. She wanted to know what he was thinking when he sat in silence looking out the bus windows; she wanted to know what he dreamed about at night. She wanted to hear all about his mom, his school, and his neighborhood near the beach . . .

She lifted her head as footsteps approached. She didn't need to be told Liane was coming near; she could smell the light scent of her friend's perfume.

Paige's hands froze on the keyboard as Liane chirped a greeting. Though she couldn't see what Liane was doing, she could picture her leaning over Noah, one hand on the back of the bench seat, the other maybe resting on Noah's shoulder . . .

"We're working." Irritation sharpened Paige's voice.

"I can see that." Liane's tone was as smooth as butter. "What I heard sounds good."

"We're just getting started," Noah said, probably looking up at Liane. "Hey, what do you think about the chorus? Should we sing it in harmony, or do some kind of handoff—you know, I sing a line, you sing a line, Paige sings a line—"

Paige cleared her throat. "Excuse me, Noah, but we're never going to get any work done if you keep asking Liane's opinion about every little thing."

The atmosphere filled with silence for a long moment, then Liane said, "I think I'll go back to reading my book. You guys are busy."

Paige felt her cheeks burn as she dipped her chin. She wasn't usually so catty, but being cooped up in a bus with the same people all the time could frazzle a girl's nerves.

As Noah strummed the chorus, she would have given her last dollar to see his face. Was he angry? sad? Did he hate her, or had he even noticed how snappish she'd been?

He began to sing, but the enthusiasm had gone out of his voice.

"Now now now, I'm trusting heaven alone,
Now I'm thinkin' 'bout another home,
Now I'm trading in my heart of stone,
I'm trusting heaven . . . heaven alone."

Paige followed him on the keyboard, automatically working in the chord changes, then lifted her hands from the keys and turned in his direction. "The chorus begins with a G chord," she said, keeping her tone light and smooth.

She couldn't let him know about the festering jealousy that made her heart ache whenever Liane was around. She couldn't let him know that she liked him more than the other guys in the group. All she could do was stick to their project and treat him as a friend.

She turned her head when he didn't respond. "You writing this down?"

"Yeah," he answered. "I'm writing."

"Good. Now, from the G chord, I think we might come up with an interesting switch if we move to an E minor with the B in the bass . . ."

Noah did not respond, and Paige wondered if she'd completely lost his respect.

12

As Paige's fingers roamed over the keyboard, Noah watched in silent amazement. The girl had the concentration of a laser beam, and nothing seemed to distract her. She'd acted a little snippy when Liane came over, but all geniuses were touchy, weren't they?

"It's good if we can vary the rhythms," she was saying now, her fingers flying over the black and whites as she improvised a rhythmic accompaniment. "And I like the way you repeated the word *now* in the chorus—repetition is always good. Makes the song easier to sing and remember."

Noah propped his chin in his hand. "Uh-huh."

"Here's a thought—listen to this and tell me what you think."

She raised her hands, laced her fingers together, then cracked her knuckles. When he laughed, she sent

Noah

him a smile. "I was beginning to wonder if you were still awake."

"I'm awake—and I'm amazed at you. You're incredible."

Two bright red spots colored her pale cheeks as she placed her hands on the keyboard. Then she began to play the chorus, but instead of the strict four beats per measure he'd used, she played it in a more gentle rhythm:

"Now—now now, I'm trusting heaven,
Now—now now, I'm thinkin' of home,
Now—now now, I'm trading my heart of stone,
Now—I'm trusting heaven . . . heaven alone."

She lifted her hands. "That's an alternative—sorta like a waltz, though, isn't it?"

"Yeah." He shook his head. "I don't think we want a waltz . . . although I can't believe the way you can just change things like that."

She shrugged again. "I think you're right—I don't much like it in three. Okay—so we'll keep it in four. That's better, I think. And we'll do the rest of it that way, but with a different drive in the rhythm—"

On an impulse, Noah leaned forward and kissed her cheek. "Thanks, Paige, for doing this for me."

Paige didn't move for a moment, then her hand slowly rose to the side of her face.

Seeing her embarrassment, Noah cleared his throat. "Sorry. I thought—well, I just wanted to thank you for doing this. You're amazing . . . I can't believe you'd want to help a beginner like me."

She pressed her lips together, and for a moment he wished she would take off her glasses so he could look in her eyes for some clue about her feelings. But Paige hardly ever took off her glasses, and her feelings tended to come out through her music, not her face.

"No need to apologize," she said, her voice cracking. "That was the sort of thing any brother might do for a sister, right?"

"Right." Noah leaned back and laughed. "Well, maybe not *any* brother and sister. My friends back home are more likely to throttle their sisters than to . . . well, do that."

Paige lowered her head, her cheeks brightening as her fingers flowed over the keys, producing a sweet melody he'd never heard before. "That's okay," she said, bending lower. "I think I understand what you're feeling."

Noah nodded, grateful that at least one of them did. He didn't have a clue what he was feeling these days.

13

Paige waited until she heard the creak of the leatherette cushions as Noah stood and left, then she stopped playing and covered her burning face with her hands.

He had *kissed* her! It wasn't a boyfriend's kiss or anything like that, and he'd agreed when she said it was something a brother might do for a sister. Still . . . none of the other guys had ever kissed her. And Shane, who *was* her brother, probably hadn't kissed her since he was four or five.

What did it mean?

She and Noah had grown closer after that night in the broken elevator—she seemed to spend every free minute thinking about him, and maybe he'd been thinking of her, too. Or maybe not. He was still close to Liane—those two had always hung together—but he'd spent more time

Noah

with Paige in the last few days than he'd spent with her since they'd begun touring.

And he was beginning to appreciate her special gift for composing. Everyone in YB2 had natural talent—even Taz could sing. But she had a gift for composing, and most of the time the other singers saw only the results of her hard work. Noah had witnessed her talent unfolding; she had let him watch a private part of her life . . . and he'd been impressed. She'd heard approval in his voice, felt it in the brief pressure of his lips on her cheek . . .

He'd kissed her!

She squinched her eyes shut, suddenly grateful for her dark glasses that kept the world at a safe distance. No one could see the expression behind her glasses, no one could know how hard she was resisting the urge to scream, to run up and down the bus, to cry out and tell the world she thought Noah Dudash was the most fascinating guy in the world . . .

She couldn't do any of those things. She couldn't speak of her feelings even to Liane, her roommate and closest friend.

She couldn't tell Shane 'cause he'd laugh at her, and she couldn't tell her father or Aunt Rhonda because they'd feel duty-bound to warn her about the "no couples" rule.

So she'd have to carry this feeling like a seed in the depths of her heart. And in time, with a little watering, a little feeding, and some sunlight, maybe the feeling would grow into something beautiful.

Or maybe it would shrivel and die. Who could say?

She pressed her hand over her heart. For now, she would protect this feeling and keep it safe . . . and secret.

14

Monday, October 11

A shiver of excitement rippled through Paige's arms
when Larry announced that they were taking I-40 into
metropolitan Nashville. Paige loved Nashville. The city
had always excited her—not only was it the home of
country music, but it had become the eastern home of
almost *all* music. Because the area had been populated
by hundreds of studios and thousands of musicians, she
felt at home the instant Larry whooped and said they
had just crossed the city limits.

They'd been invited to sing at the Country Music
Awards, another nationally televised awards program.
While some reviewers were scratching their heads at the
invitation, Paige knew the group had been tapped for the
honor because their first album included "Never Forget,"
a song about all the soldiers who had given their lives for

America's freedom. Country music fans loved America, and so did YB2.

YB2 had been scheduled to sing "Never Forget" on the show, and Paige was grateful they'd be performing one of their quieter, more reflective songs. No hip-hop choreography or stage-stomping rhythms. Just a good reminder for Americans.

A short while after their arrival in Music City USA, Larry stopped the bus and announced that they'd reached their destination. Because their current concert program didn't include "Never Forget," RC had rented a banquet room at the Hyatt Regency to serve as a rehearsal hall. The hotel had promised to post extra security outside the double doors in case word of the group's presence managed to leak, but as Paige stepped off the bus and lifted her face to the sun, everything seemed quiet and peaceful.

They checked in, unloaded luggage, and took a few minutes to unpack. RC wanted to begin rehearsing as soon as possible, so at 2 p.m. sharp, Paige walked with Liane from their room to the rehearsal room, then took a seat at the piano. While the others listened to Taz explain the taped marks on the floor, Paige lifted her head and tried to get a sense of the room. The place was carpeted, which would make choreography a little difficult to practice, and the metallic chinking sounds she heard every few seconds probably came from metal chairs someone was stacking along the wall.

Or not. She stiffened as she heard a chair knock the

edge of her keyboard. "Sorry," Shane said, moving his chair to her right. So—they were setting up in the standard YB2 semicircle. Shane would be seated at her right hand, while Liane sat at her left. Noah always sat next to Liane, while Josiah took the position at the end of the arc.

"Paige?"

She lifted her head as Taz called out. "Yes?"

"How are those levels for you? Can you hear the piano in the monitor?"

"Yeah, Taz, thanks. It sounds great."

A moment later the door opened and closed again, shutting with a metallic clack. She heard her father's greeting and the newcomer's reply.

She placed the voice immediately: Lew Hargrave, a vice president for Melisma Records and YB2's official contact with the company.

Of course he would be here—though he worked in Los Angeles, Melisma maintained a Nashville office so they could remain in the thick of the industry.

"Hey, everyone!" Lew moved down the line, shaking hands and saying hello to each of the others. A moment later Paige felt his hand close around hers—he never shook her hand, he just grabbed it and squeezed, as if a blind girl couldn't be trusted to manage a proper handshake.

"Hey, Paige!" Lew's voice was bright. "How's our little Mo-zart doing?"

He couldn't even pronounce *Mozart* correctly. There was supposed to be a *T* sound in the middle.

"I'm fine." She gave him a polite smile. "And you?"

"Doin' great—as are your records. The new one's already gone platinum, have you heard?"

"We heard." She nodded. "Thanks for the update."

"Hey, Shane, my man!" As Lew moved down the line, Paige drew a deep breath and hoped rehearsal would begin soon.

Fortunately, she didn't have to wait long. As soon as Lew finished his greetings, RC rapped on the director's stand with his baton. "Okay, gang, let's get 'Never Forget' ready," he said. "Joe—you're the only one who doesn't know this number, but I'm sure you'll catch on quickly. But I also have a surprise for all of you."

Paige's internal antennae perked up.

"Lew," RC continued, "has been talking to the CMA folks, and they've decided they'd like another song. Trouble is, we don't really have anything else that fits the country music style. I was trying to figure out how we could adapt something, when I realized we've had the perfect song for some time."

"What song is that?" Liane asked.

Paige heard a smile enter her father's voice. "Noah's new song. I heard Noah and Paige playing it on the bus the other day, and I think it'll be perfect. Noah, Paige— what do you say?"

Paige felt her throat go dry. Perform Noah's song tomorrow night? On national television?

She turned her head toward the chairs to her left. "Noah?"

"Oh, man." His voice rasped. "Um . . . I'm not sure we can do it, RC."

"Sure you can," Taz called from the soundboard. "It sounds nice with just keyboard and guitar. Kind of a folksy feel."

Noah didn't sound convinced, so Paige jumped in. "I'm game, but only if Noah is. After all, it's his song."

"Noah?" RC asked. "It's your decision."

Silence sifted down like snowfall, then Noah cleared his throat. "Okay, sure, if you think we're ready. I wouldn't want to do anything you don't like, though."

"That's why we're here, Noah. I want you and Paige to sing your song for Lew. I think he's going to be pleasantly surprised by what you guys have managed to put together in your free time."

"You mean . . . you want us to sing it now?"

"Yep." RC's chair creaked as he stood. "Here's your guitar—I brought it off the bus myself."

"Lots of country music fans love guitars," Liane added helpfully. "This song is bound to be a hit."

Silently wishing Liane would hush up, Paige improvised a few opening bars. She heard the sound of a chair being dragged across carpet, then Noah's voice whispered in her ear. "Are we ready for this?"

She nodded. "Just pretend we're on the bus. I think we'll be fine."

And then, while everyone watched and listened, she began to play for real and Noah joined in. He sang the verses; she joined him in light harmony on the choruses.

No one else chimed in; no one sought to steal the spotlight.

After the last guitar strum, Paige straightened at the piano bench. The others applauded and whistled so loudly that Paige grinned in pleased surprise. Noah had to be beaming . . . what a great reception for his song.

When the cheering died down, RC spoke. "Well, Lew? What do you think?"

The record producer cleared his throat. "Yeah . . . the song's good for country, all right, so I'll go along with your idea. But I don't think I'd put it in your concert program. It's a downer. Too depressing."

"But that's the point," Noah interrupted. "It's not meant to be depressing. The guy in the song realizes he won't be depressed if he trusts heaven for what happens next—"

"Calm down, kid, it's a good song. And the rednecks who love that sappy stuff will eat it up. But it's not a YB2 song."

Paige heard the jingle of coins, followed by the sound of someone's shoes retreating across the carpet.

"Keep writing music," Lew said, and from the distance of his voice Paige figured he was standing near the door. "Sing this one at the CMA, then go back to your drawing board and write us something livelier and more upbeat. Then you'll be writing something YB2 can really use."

She heard the click of the door latch as it opened.

"Gotta run, group, but I'll see you tomorrow night

before the show. Break a leg and all that stuff! I'll catch you later."

Then he was gone.

For Noah's sake, Paige was glad Lew hadn't wanted to stick around.

15

When the trio of TV cameras turned toward him and
the lights dimmed, Noah felt as though he had swallowed
a living eel that was now wallowing in his gut. He'd
been a little nervous when the group performed "Never
Forget"—after all, it wasn't one of their regular songs and
they hadn't sung it in several months. Plus, it had about
a thousand words and several verses about brave men and
women who had died in battles defending America.

But that nervousness was nothing compared to what
he felt now as he stood in the spotlight with his guitar
on his knee. At least he wasn't alone. Paige stood at the
piano only a few inches away, marooned with him in that
circle of light.

She played a measure; he joined in with a broken
guitar chord. Finally, he drew a deep breath and began
to sing:

"I thought life would sorta flow by,
I never had much reason to cry,
Until you left me alone."

He began to tremble as the words poured from his
heart. He had scarcely uttered the first few lines of the
first verse when a picture of Justus flashed in his mind
and a lump rose in his throat—

He'd never get through this song without crying if
he thought about his dog. Jussy had only been gone a
few weeks, and he still couldn't talk about him without
choking up.

So he'd have to think about something else. He sang
the rest of the first verse while thinking about his father:

"I thought I'd caught the golden ring,
Life offered me so many things,
Until my heart turned to stone."

His heart *had* turned to stone when his dad left, and
it was only beginning to soften a little. So he couldn't
think about his dad either, especially not now. Instead
he could think about the millions of people who might
be watching on TV—oops, that thought made his toes
curl—or he could think about the unblinking red eye
of the camera in the center aisle.

Was his father watching?

Pushing that thought aside, he focused on the
camera.

Noah

"Now now now, I'm trusting heaven alone,
Now I'm thinkin' 'bout another home,
Now I'm trading in my heart of stone,
I'm trusting heaven . . . heaven alone."

He tilted his head, almost surprised when Paige joined him on the chorus. He'd been concentrating so hard on that red light he'd almost forgotten that she stood beside him. But like a true friend, she was there, backing him up and making him sound a lot better than he was.

She wouldn't let him fail. If his throat clogged up and he started to bawl in front of all America, Paige would take over and keep on singing. The camera would shift to her, and she'd smile and carry on like she always did. She'd save the show—and Noah's reputation—because that's what friends did.

He smiled as he remembered her confidence in rehearsal. She liked the song, and she'd believed in it all along. If she believed he could pull if off . . . maybe he could.

With new energy Noah kept playing and plunged into the second verse.

16

Paige had no idea how they looked under the TV lights, but Noah's song came off without a hitch. And afterward, when the camera pulled away to focus on the emcees standing at the far right of the stage, Noah took her hand and led her offstage. When they were safely away from public scrutiny, he dropped his guitar, wrapped her in a bear hug, and swung her around in a circle.

Breathless, he set her down. "Thanks, Paige! I never could have done it without you!"

"You're welcome!" She struggled to breathe in his tight embrace, then felt a twinge of disappointment when he released her. "Who knows, Noah? Maybe some recording big shot will hear your song and want to record it."

"Aw, I don't care about that." He took her elbow; she let him lead her away from the hubbub into the wings. "I'm just relieved we pulled it off without flubbing up.

I've never played guitar on TV before. I was afraid my fingers would slip or something."

"You did fine," Paige reassured him. "Actually, we all did fine tonight. There are so many words to 'Never Forget,' I was terrified I'd forget a verse or two, maybe leave out a couple of our major American heroes."

Together they laughed.

"I see the others," Noah said, leaning closer as he guided her through the backstage area. "They're waiting at the end of this hall, next to the restrooms. And if you don't mind, I think I need to duck into the men's room."

"Me, too—I mean, I could use the ladies' room. Can you put me in front of the right door?"

"Sure—and I don't see Liane with the others, so she must be inside. Just call out for her once you get in so she can point you in the right direction."

Paige followed until Noah placed her hands on a wooden door, then she pushed her way into the room.

A second swinging door lay right beyond this one, so she pushed it open, too, then stood in the center of a room that echoed when she called Liane's name.

A soft southern voice answered. "Do you need help, honey? I'm not Liane, but maybe I can help."

Paige lowered her head and smiled. "I'm sorry. I thought my friend was in here."

"It's jest me 'n you, from what I can tell. You need me to . . . lead you somewhere?"

Paige laughed. "If you can point me to a stall, I think I can take it from there."

"No problem, sugar. By the way, I heard your songs—both of 'em. You and that young man sounded real nice together."

A few minutes later, Paige came out of the stall. The sound of running water drew her to the sink, and as she washed her hands she heard the woman's soft voice again. "I think you're pretty amazin', girl. They tell me you write a lot of your group's music."

"Me and my brother and my dad. It's kind of a family thing."

"Well, sure sounds like you've got a good thing goin' on." A smile crept into the woman's voice. "Did you write the song you and that boy sang?"

"No, that was Noah's song. He wrote it by himself—I just helped with the arrangement. It was pretty simple, really."

"That's why it was so beautiful. Sometimes the best songs are the simplest." The woman turned the water off; then Paige heard the *click* of a paper towel dispenser. "You two looked awful cute together."

Paige lowered her head as her cheeks began to burn.

The woman moved close enough for Paige to smell her sweet perfume. "Tell me, sugar—is it love?"

"*What?*"

"Between you two young folks—are you sweethearts?"

Her cheeks must be scarlet by now! Paige tipped her head back, wishing she knew the answer to the woman's question. "It's not supposed to be love. We're not allowed to date while we're on the road."

"Who's talking about *datin'*? Music is about emotions, honey, and by the sound of your music I know you feel 'em. So—is it love?"

Paige managed a trembling smile. They were alone, no one was listening, and she didn't know this woman. But she couldn't be a reporter, because they were barred from this backstage area, so why not take a chance and ask a perfectly innocent question?

"How do you know," she whispered, "when it's love?"

The woman chuckled. "Land sakes, honey, if you can answer that, you'll have the world eatin' out of your hand. It's uncertainty that makes the world go round—half the songs in the music industry are about mistaken love, false love, confused love. The only thing I can tell you for sure is that it'd sure *better* be love when you say 'I do.' Until then, you're better off just callin' it infatuation."

Paige nodded as the bathroom door creaked open. "Paige? Oh."

Liane. Paige heard Liane politely greet the other woman, then the woman's shoes—probably high heels—clicked over the tiles.

"I gotta go, hon," she called, pulling the bathroom door open. "But I wish you the best of luck—and I'll be lookin' for you in the years ahead."

Paige pulled a paper towel from the rack, then heard Liane panting in her ear. "Ohmigoodness! Did you see—did you realize who you were talking to?"

Paige shrugged. "Some nice Southern lady."

"Some nice—Paige Clawson, I can't believe you're so clueless. You were talking to Terri Su Scoggins in the flesh. Good grief, I can't *believe* you didn't ask for her autograph!"

Paige froze for a moment. Terri Su Scoggins? The woman was a legend not only in country music, but in the international music industry. She'd written more than two hundred hit songs and earned a fortune recording her own albums. She had to be at least fifty, but her voice still sounded young.

Paige turned toward the door. "Why didn't *you* ask her for an autograph? *You* saw her."

"Well—why—I was just surprised to find Terri Su Scoggins in the bathroom! I didn't know people like her ever stepped inside public toilets. And she was talking to you! What'd she say?"

A small smile lifted the corner of Paige's mouth as she dropped her hand to Liane's arm. "She said she enjoyed our music. Now—can we please leave? I don't want to spend all night in the bathroom."

Sighing like a genuine drama queen, Liane led her out.

17

Noah, who never could go back to sleep once he'd been shocked into consciousness by his shrill alarm clock, tossed his luggage into the bus bay at 4 a.m., then climbed into the bus seats and pulled a few new comic books from his book bag. Larry had picked them up at the grocery store on last night's munchie run.

They'd been on the road for a couple of hours by the time the sun rose and tinted the highway a golden bronze. He heard stirrings from the bunk area, and the sounds of the girls whispering. At the front of the bus, Larry celebrated the sunrise by tuning in to a country station and jacking up the volume.

A few minutes later, Noah looked up from his comic book as Liane sank into the seat next to him. He looked at her, waiting to see if she wanted something, but she didn't meet his gaze. She just sat there, casually nibbling from a box of stale popcorn, keeping her eyes on the front of the bus.

Who could understand women? Noah returned to his reading. A few minutes later, though, Liane nudged him with her elbow.

"Hey! That hurt!"

"Oh, it did not."

"Did too. Your elbows are like spears."

"Shhh." She crouched lower in the seat. "Paige just walked by."

He looked toward the front and saw Paige's brown hair above the back of one of the front seats. "So?"

"I think she'll be coming back this way again in a minute."

Noah frowned, trying to figure out why Paige-watching was so important. The bathroom was located at the back of the bus, and nobody ever made a big deal of going back there—

"I don't want her to hear me," Liane whispered, sinking lower into the seat.

"Hear you *what?*"

Liane didn't answer, but after a minute Paige did come back down the aisle, one hand reaching out to feel her way through the seat section, the other hand holding her toiletries bag. She was probably planning to brush her teeth and wash her face . . . no big deal.

Noah leaned over Liane's knees and looked down the

aisle. Paige had disappeared, but the bathroom door now read "occupied."

"Okay." He straightened in the seat. "She can't hear you. So what's up?"

Liane grinned at him like a little kid who had just robbed the cookie jar. "I've got a secret."

"What?"

"I probably shouldn't tell you."

He shrugged. "Then don't."

"But it might be important. And I don't want Paige to get in trouble."

"Excuse me, are you talking about Paige Clawson? She doesn't get into trouble. Ever."

"Nobody's perfect, Noah. Not even Paige."

He waited a minute, but Liane seemed determined to prolong the suspense. She dropped another mouthful of popcorn into her mouth, then grinned at him. "She'f got a crupfh of youfh."

He stared at her. "Try it without the popcorn."

Liane swallowed, then checked the aisle to be sure the coast was still clear. "I said—" she turned back to face him—"I think she's got a crush on you."

Noah laughed. "Fat chance."

"No, seriously. Haven't you noticed the way she's suddenly been paying attention to you?"

He picked up his comic book. "Paige doesn't pay much attention to anyone. She can't see them."

"No, but still . . . I don't know if I can explain it, but I can tell. She sorta perks up whenever you come into

Young Believer on Tour 101

Noah

the room. And we've always gotten along great, but lately I've felt a little . . . tension coming from her. I think she's jealous."

Noah dropped his book. "Now you're really talking crazy."

"I know, I know, that's why it's so unbelievable. I mean, there's nothing going on between you and me—"

"Absolutely nothing."

"But we're still really good friends. And I think she resents that."

"How can you tell?"

"Well . . . remember the other day when you guys were working on your song? She nearly bit my head off when you started talking to me."

He shook his head. "She was concentrating. She's very focused."

"Yeah—on you."

"Not true."

"Yes, it is."

"No—and you have no proof."

Liane waited a minute, then bit her fingernail. "Yeah . . . maybe I do."

Noah lifted his comic book and tried to read. This was not a good conversation; it could wreck his relationship with both girls. Still . . . he couldn't help but wonder.

"Okay." He turned to Liane, then leaned over her and double-checked to be sure Paige wasn't coming down the aisle. "What's your proof?"

Liane giggled. "She talks in her sleep."

"Get out."

"No, it's true! And guess who she's been talking about the last four nights?"

Groaning, Noah buried his head in his hand. He did *not* need this, not now.

"You!" Liane squealed the word. "She's been talking about you!"

Like a jack-in-the-box, Josiah popped over the seat in front of them. "Who's been talking about Noah?"

Noah glared at Liane. "Now you've done it. This is how rumors get started." He waved at Josiah. "Nobody's talking about anybody, so please turn around."

The younger boy lifted a brow, then grinned. "Ohhhhh, no need to take out an ad. I should just chill, right?"

"Right!" Liane and Noah spoke in unison.

When Josiah had disappeared behind the seat, Noah lowered his voice. "Um . . . what was she saying?"

"I can't really figure it out," Liane admitted, "and I don't think it makes much sense, but your name comes up a lot."

Noah shrugged. "I'm sure it's no big deal. If she's really saying my name, it's probably because we've been working on my song a lot." He grinned. "Did I tell you RC is thinking about adding it to the concert program? He said it might be nice to have something low-key between the first and second halves. So while the rest of you are changing costumes, Paige and I are gonna stay onstage and do my song, just guitar and piano. RC said he thought it'd be a nice way to change gears and go into the break."

Liane rolled her eyes. "I'm thrilled for you."

"You are not."

"I am—but I think you're missing the point. Paige works with everybody, but she doesn't talk about any of the rest of us in her sleep."

Noah let his head fall to the window. "I still think you're imagining things."

"Oh yeah? Well, remember that I'm telling you this to warn you to be careful not to lead her on or anything. Paige is awesome, and you wouldn't want to hurt her feelings."

No, he wouldn't . . . especially when her father was the group's director.

Noah and Liane both flinched when they heard the bathroom door close. Paige had to be coming this way.

"Be careful!" Liane hissed, standing to go back to her own seat.

Noah accepted her warning silently, then picked up his comic book to hide the heat stealing over his face. Paige couldn't see it, of course, but he wondered if she might *sense* his embarrassment as she walked by. She seemed to sense everything else.

Bringing the book down so only his eyes were revealed, he peered over the edge as Paige felt her way back to her usual place at the front of the bus. She wore a small, practiced smile, and her hands lightly touched the back of each seat as she walked by. He wondered if she would speak when she passed him, but she didn't; she just kept walking toward the front.

Liane had to be wrong. A girl in love would have stopped to say something. She'd be hanging around all goggle-eyed like the fans who dangled out of car windows and screamed when the YB2 bus rolled by.

But . . . what if Liane was right? He liked Paige and thought she was great. But she wasn't like a real girl—well, she *was* a real girl, but she wasn't the kind the guys back at his school asked out. Paige was the kind of girl that everyone thought needed to be protected from life.

Liane, on the other hand, was a rough-and-tumble girl. You could play flag football with her and never have a worry. You could take her to a movie or a concert and laugh and scream and toss popcorn onto the people in the rows in front of you . . .

He couldn't imagine doing any of those things with Paige.

So . . . whether or not Liane was right, he might be smart to back off a bit. He and Paige had been spending a lot of time together, so maybe it was good his song was finished. He could let things slide back to the way they used to be.

That way, no one would get hurt.

Especially not him.

18

"Paige." Her father spoke in a sharp tone that cut through the growl of the diesel engines beneath the hulking bus. "Play Noah's part, please, beginning with 'and the rockets' red glare.' He's not getting it."

She lowered her chin as something within her shriveled in sympathy for Noah. They were scheduled to sing "The Star-Spangled Banner" at the opening game of the World Series in less than two hours, but Noah's heart didn't seem to be into the work of learning RC's five-part *a cappella* arrangement. He was singing more quietly than usual, and he had missed a couple of important notes.

She plucked out his part on the keyboard, then dropped her hands into her lap as her father tapped the tabletop with his baton. "Okay, from the top. On four. Ready? One, two, three."

Paige drew a deep breath, then sang. She couldn't see her dad's waving hands, but she could hear her friends' breaths around the bus tables. When she played the piano, she set her tempo to match the click of RC's baton; when they sang *a cappella,* she had to listen carefully to avoid mistakes.

Singing *a cappella* forced them to make one other adjustment. When they sang with a prerecorded musical track, they cut off their notes on a certain beat and held their positions until Shane yelled "cut." But they didn't move when they sang *a cappella,* and there were no rhythmic beats to count. Someone needed to do something visual to cut them off at the same time, and since Paige couldn't see, she'd been selected to nod her head and direct the final cut.

They sang through the arrangement more smoothly this time, and Paige was happy to hear Noah get the tricky tenor part. The tempo slowed at the ending, and at the final "and the home—of the—brave," Paige counted six beats, then jerked her head downward in a nod.

"Perfect!" RC clapped his hands. "Great cutoff, everybody. Great job." Paige heard him change position as the bus shifted gears and lurched forward.

"We're in New York," Shane called from the window. "Wow. Look at that skyline!"

"I don't know how you can see anything," Liane remarked, her voice coming from the other side of the bus. "All I see is buildings and bridges."

Paige said nothing as she powered off her portable

keyboard. Long ago she had accepted that the others would get excited over things she'd never be able to see, not even in her imagination. When she was younger, she used to demand that Shane or her dad or Aunt Rhonda describe what they were seeing.

These days she sat and waited, remaining in the dark until someone remembered her.

"Cool!"

She heard Josiah's exclamation from the window to her right. "What do you see, Joe?" she asked quietly.

"Oh, man—more buildings than I've ever seen in my life! We're going over this huge bridge right now—I'm looking for the Statue of Liberty, but I don't see it."

From somewhere up ahead, Noah laughed. "The Statue's not here, Joe—it's out in New York Harbor. Maybe we'll have a chance to catch it later."

"I sure hope so." Josiah's voice dropped to a lower note. "I'd hate to come all the way to New York City and not see the Statue of Liberty."

Paige said nothing, but his words grated on her nerves. She'd been going places all her life without see-ing *anything*.

And Noah ignoring her . . . well, it hurt. For the last couple of days he'd been acting strange, a little distant. After their successful performance at the CMA, she'd thought they were closer friends than ever, but Noah had barely spoken to her since Nashville.

Paige had no idea why. Had she done something? *Not* done something? Had she said something to hurt his feelings or embarrass him? Maybe she hadn't said something, hadn't bragged on him enough.

"Oh, no." From the front of the bus, Liane groaned.

Paige's inner alarm bells rang. "What?"

"It's going to rain." Disappointment soaked Liane's voice. "We're going to be standing out in the middle of Shea Stadium in the rain."

Taz groaned. "Man, the sound equipment's going to get wet."

"Doesn't matter," RC said, his voice matter-of-fact. "You know what they say—the show must go on."

"Maybe the rain will stop," Shane said. "I think I see some blue sky over in the east."

Shane's patch of blue sky had completely disappeared by the time the game began. And as they huddled in the Mets' covered dugout, Paige could feel the mist of rain on her face.

"It's raining a bit," RC told them, "but not enough to call the game, so we're going to go ahead and sing. Everybody miked up?"

Paige automatically felt for the battery pack at her waist. The tiny mike hung from her ear; its sensitive tip bent toward her mouth. From a distance of only a few feet, the mike was all but invisible.

"Okay, then." She heard the sound of RC rubbing his hands together. "Shane, make sure you escort Paige out and watch out for slippery grass. Look for my signal when it's time to sing—and have fun out there, you guys!"

Paige slipped her arm through her brother's, then felt her heart skip a beat as he stepped from concrete onto the soft expanse of—what was this, dirt? A moment later she smelled the sweet scent of wet grass. They had dressed in jeans, red-white-and-blue shirts, and ball caps—Aunt Rhonda's version of baseball costumes.

"Here you go." Shane planted Paige in a spot, then moved to stand by her right side. Just for today, Noah stood at her left, followed by Liane and Josiah, forming a tight semicircle.

Paige shivered as she breathed in the chilly air. They would have to stand here for a few minutes, long enough for the TV people to move through their announcements and secure their camera shots. To take her mind off the numbing cold, Paige lifted her head and listened to the rowdy crowd. "Are they looking at us?" she asked her brother.

"Not yet," Shane answered. "I mean, sure, some of them may be looking, but the announcers are busy with other things. The camera operators are still messing around."

She said nothing, but shivered as the light rain continued to fall.

"Finally," Shane whispered under his breath. "I think it's show time."

"And now," the announcer's voice suddenly blared through the speakers, "here to open the first game of this year's World Series—YB2! Would you please stand for the singing of our national anthem?"

Paige hummed an F, their starting pitch, then Shane counted off: "One, two, three."

"Oh, say can you see . . ."

As an intense silence settled over the crowd, Paige was amazed at the clear sound of their voices over the speakers. In some ways, this appearance was more exciting than one of their concerts—they were making history, they were taking part in a national legacy. How cool was that?

They hit the last note, held it for eight beats, then Paige jerked her head. An instant of silence rang through the rain, then the stadium erupted in wild applause and the sound of stamping feet.

"We're outta here," Shane said, reaching for Paige's hand. They hustled off the field as quickly as they could, then Paige dropped Shane's hand and stumbled, breathless, into the dugout—and discovered that it had filled with baseball players.

"Excuse me, little lady," one man said after she smacked into him. "Here, let me help you out of this box."

"I've got her." Ever protective, Shane grabbed Paige's hand again and tugged her forward. Paige followed, wishing that it had been Noah who had noticed her predicament.

Flustered and fumbling, she followed Shane through some sort of hall or tunnel where every sound echoed and bounced back to their ears.

Finally they arrived at a dry, quiet space.

"Great job, group." RC moved around the circle, congratulating everyone with hugs and pats on the back. "Here, let's get you out of those microphones and into some warm jackets. How cold was it out there?"

"Cold enough," Paige said, shivering. Someone—probably her dad—draped a jacket around her shoulders.

"Wow!" Noah's voice rang with surprise. "Mets jackets? For all of us?"

"The Mets' manager thought it'd be a nice gift," RC said. "I told him I knew you'd love 'em."

"Man, I can't get the zipper to open," Noah said, and from the sound of his voice Paige knew he was standing right in front of her.

"Here," she said, putting out her hand. "I'm good at undoing zippers." She waited expectantly, with a smile on her face, but Noah didn't answer. After a moment she lowered her hand, not wanting to look like a fool staring at nothing.

So . . . Noah not only didn't want her help, he wanted to ignore her completely. Fine. She could live with that if she had to. But the one thing she couldn't live with was the not knowing why he had decided to back off from their friendship.

What had she done to upset him, and why didn't he have the simple decency to talk to her about it?

19

With an effort, Noah rolled over in the narrow bunk and tried to force his eyes to stay open. He peered into the thin gray light of morning, swallowed, and confirmed what his brain had been trying to tell him since sometime in the middle of the night—his throat killed.

He swallowed again and winced. Sore throats and colds were a singer's worst enemy, and YB2 had endured several cases since beginning their tour two years ago. The best cure was rest, hot chicken soup, and a warm scarf around the throat.

But when a group had only five singers, they couldn't afford the luxury of bed rest. Noah would have to sing tonight and act as though nothing was wrong, but at least he could rest on the bus. Maybe he'd curl back into his bunk after they stopped for breakfast. He could sleep

Noah

for the rest of the day, or at least until they pulled into the loading dock of the next civic center or auditorium.

Wait—tonight was the gig in Las Vegas. Which meant his dad would be there, which meant he'd be singing with a sore throat for the man who hadn't heard him sing in over five years . . .

Oh, man. Why was he getting sick on this day of all days?

Since singing at the World Series, they'd been pushing forward on the road, rushing to head west in time for the Las Vegas concert. They'd gotten the World Series invitation months before, but until the end of the baseball season, no one knew exactly where those games would be played. RC had been hoping the first game would be played out west, but the Mets had clinched their division championship and the first game had been held in New York City.

Which meant poor Larry was driving fourteen hours a day, and RC was filling in while Larry tried to catch a few hours of sleep in the bus.

The other singers were restless with boredom. After a while the view from the window stopped offering much entertainment value, and Noah had already read all the comic books Larry had picked up at the last grocery store. Liane had a stack of novels she'd offered to let him borrow, but her books were all too long and too complicated looking. Josiah had his handheld video games, but Noah always beat him.

He had played his guitar until his fingers hurt, confronted Shane in a mean game of tic-tac-toe, and sung along with Larry to the country music station. He had clipped his nails, taken his vitamins, and gotten a full ten hours of sleep for the last couple of nights. He and Liane had stared out the window and tried to find cars with license plates from all fifty states, but that had become impossible when they realized they weren't likely to find any Hawaiian tags in the Midwest.

Yessir, Noah had tried to stay as busy as he could . . . mainly because he didn't want to think about his dad picking up those tickets for the Vegas concert.

He had called the ticket booth at the MGM Grand Garden Arena the day before the Country Music Awards. A nice lady had identified herself as Irene and asked how she could help.

"Yes, um, I'm Noah Dudash from YB2, and I'd like to have two tickets left for my father at the will-call window."

She'd laughed in his ear. "Nice try, kid. Buh-bye."

"No—wait! I really am Noah Dudash—and listen, I can prove it. You can charge these to our account or whatever, and the contact will be Rhonda Clawson of Orlando, Florida."

Irene hesitated. "Really."

"Yes. If you check, you'll see I'm telling the truth."

"Hang on a minute, kid."

He'd heard the sounds of rustling papers, then something had clicked and strains of elevator music filled his ear. A minute later, though, Irene came back on the line.

"Why, Mr. Dudash—sorry for the trouble. Now, who did you want these tickets for?"

"Bill Dudash and—well, whoever he wants to bring."

"He's your father?"

"Yes."

"That's nice." Her voice warmed. "Are you sure you don't want to have the tickets sent to his house? We could do that for you. Mail or delivery, whichever you prefer."

"I don't think so. I don't know where he lives, and . . . well, I'm not sure he'll show up. If the tickets aren't used, YB2 doesn't get charged, right?"

"I'm not sure, but I'll ask."

"Okay. Whatever."

Silence hummed over the line for a moment, then the woman's voice softened. "How long's it been since you've seen your daddy?"

He knew he ought to be irritated by her snooping, but Irene reminded him of his mother's sister. She was always asking him questions, and when she asked with a smile, he couldn't help but answer.

"Um . . . five years."

"That's too long."

"Yeah, it is."

"Okay, Noah—oops, forgot to ask. What kind of tickets do you want for Mr. Dudash? Stadium seats, balcony, or floor?"

Noah scratched his head. He had decided to be nice to his father, but how nice did he have to be?

"What would you suggest?"

Irene laughed. "Well, a lot of the best seats are sold out. You could put him in the front of the balcony if you want him to have a good look, but he'd be so far away you wouldn't be able to see him. Or you could put him on the floor—not the best seats, viewing-wise, but he'd be real close."

"I guess you could put him in the balcony. He could see everything from there, right?"

"Right."

"Then that works. Give him a couple of balcony tickets." Noah hesitated. "That's good, right?"

"Yes, honey. That's a real nice gesture."

Noah had thanked her and hung up, then scratched "Be nice to father" off his mental to-do list.

Balcony seats sounded great. His dad would have good seats, his friends would be impressed, and Noah wouldn't have to look at him. He could almost put his dad completely out of his mind, which is exactly what his dad had done with Noah since leaving for Las Vegas.

Noah lifted his head and looked toward the front of the bus. Through the dust-covered windshield he could see the brown hills of some Midwestern town, the broken line of the highway, and the back of Larry's head.

They were still miles away from Las Vegas, but they were scheduled to arrive by midday. And after the concert tonight, Noah would probably be able to forget about his dad for another five or six years.

20

Unable to sleep because of the pain in his throat, Noah pulled the blanket from his bunk and moved forward to the seats. He curled up in a pair of chairs on the left side of the bus, then propped his forehead against the glass and stared out at the countryside. The sun was up now, but it shone on a landscape so dry and barren Noah wondered how the few straggly trees and shrubs could grow in it.

They had just rolled past an interstate exit for Cedar City, Utah, when Noah felt the bus shudder. Larry grumbled behind the wheel and steered the bus to the right; within minutes the huge black machine had crawled to a stop by the side of the dusty highway.

Throughout the bus, heads lifted to attention. Everyone knew Larry was doing his best to make good time.

They also knew he wouldn't turn diesel engines off for no good reason. It took too long to get them restarted.

Larry stood and cast a quick glance down the aisle. "We've got a problem," he said flatly. "Lemme check it out."

Noah felt his stomach tighten as the man opened the door and disappeared down the steps. They couldn't have a transportation problem before a concert, especially not this one!

RC, who'd been sleeping on the lowest bunk, rose up and lumbered toward the front, then bent to peer out the windows. "Anybody see where we are?"

"Yeah." Noah rolled out of his seat and followed his director. "I saw an exit for Cedar City right before the engine died."

RC closed his eyes. "That's at least—well, I'm not sure—but I think it's at least four hours away from Vegas." As RC looked at his watch, Noah looked at the small clock mounted above the dashboard—it read 8:00 a.m. The equipment trailers had probably been in Vegas for days since they hadn't detoured to New York for the World Series.

Noah sank back in his seat. RC liked to have the singers' bus arrive by noon on concert days so they'd have time for a sound check and a last-minute rehearsal. The concert tonight was supposed to begin at eight . . . so they should be okay if Larry could get the bus fixed.

But how was he supposed to repair a bus out here in the middle of a desert?

"Larry!" RC bounded down the stairs.

Noah glanced across the bus at Liane, who had slipped into a seat near the window. Her hair was still tousled from sleep, but her eyes were sharp and awake. She pressed her hands to the glass and stared at the men on the right side of the road.

"Can you see what's happening?" Noah croaked, his hand rising to protect his sore throat.

Liane shook her head. "Not really. Larry's looking around at the motor, I think. But I don't know a thing about diesel engines."

Noah shook his head. What else could go wrong today? He might as well go back to bed and write off tonight's concert. For a minute he considered going outside and telling RC that God must be telling them they weren't supposed to perform in Las Vegas. They could let this concert slide by, have the promoters issue refunds for the tickets, and push on down the road to the next gig.

Maybe he wasn't supposed to meet his father tonight. The thought brought relief, because Noah didn't see how he could sing through a throat that felt like elves had been skateboarding on it all night long.

He looked up as RC stepped back onto the bus, then leaned on a metal support. "This," he said, seeming to speak to no one in particular, "is why I like to fly to the unscheduled shows. We never should have agreed to drive to New York. If we'd flown, we would be sitting in a Las Vegas hotel room right now, drinking coffee and eating eggs and bacon."

Noah

Noah's stomach growled at the mention of food. He hadn't realized how hungry he was.

Shane emerged from the bunks, a blanket over his shoulders and his eyes puffy. "What's going on, Dad?"

"Hurry up and wait," RC said, glancing up at his son. "It's an old philosophy, but it works. I'd rather get started early and have time to kill at the end of a job than have to break our necks to beat the clock."

Josiah peered out from behind Shane with wide eyes. "You're going to break some necks?"

RC smiled. "It's only an expression, Joe."

Shane walked stiffly toward the front. "Does Larry know what's wrong with the bus?"

RC shook his head. "He thinks air got into the fuel line somehow. He can bleed the engine and get the air out, but he has to find the hole before we can take off, or we'll be stopping again a few miles down the road." He climbed the remaining steps, then dropped into the first seat and spoke to the windshield. "Maybe it is time to get a new bus."

"We could forget the bus and fly," Shane said, his eyes glowing. "We could get a private jet. How cool would that be?"

"I like the bus." RC turned to look at his son. "Believe it or not, I believe it builds camaraderie and makes us more of a team. Besides, the stage crew has to drive. Doesn't seem fair for us to be able to fly when they're stuck on the road."

Paige emerged from the back. "What happens if we miss the concert?"

"We won't miss it. We'll start late if we have to."

"But if we're stuck here—"

"We won't be stuck. If it gets late, I'll call for a couple of cars and a U-Haul to take us to Las Vegas. But until we get down to the wire, everybody just sit tight and pray Larry finds that leak in the line."

Noah closed his eyes as RC got up and went back outside. For a second he'd been happy to think they might miss the Las Vegas concert. Thousands of fans would be disappointed, the promoters would have a fit about refunding all those tickets, and Aunt Rhonda would groan at having to reschedule such a big event.

But if they canceled, Noah wouldn't have to see his dad.

He held that thought for a moment, then frowned as a new feeling struck him—hey, he'd be disappointed not to see the man. He'd worked so hard to get to the place where he could reserve those tickets, and now he was curious about what his dad had been doing all these years.

Most of all, he wanted to see if the man in Las Vegas was anything like the man in the photos his mother had sent.

Trouble was, given the size of the stadium and the brightness of the stage lights, Noah wouldn't be able to see Bill Dudash if he sat in a balcony seat.

21

Chilled from the air conditioning that poured from an overhead vent, Paige threw a blanket over her head and snuggled into the curve of the bus seat. At least the AC was still working . . . for a while. She didn't want to think about being stranded in the desert with no transportation and no air conditioning.

"Hey." She flinched as Noah spoke and lifted the covering from her head.

"Oops." He let out an awkward laugh. "I thought you were Liane."

She tightened the blanket around her neck. "Well, I'm not."

"She must be in the bathroom—I need to talk to her."

The words stabbed at Paige's heart like a knife, but she couldn't let him see her hurt. "I can talk too, you know. I may not be a genius, but I'm no dummy."

Noah

"I never said you were." She moved over as she felt him slide into the seat next to her.

Did he mean those words as some sort of peace offering? She waited a minute, wondering what had brought him around, then lifted a brow. "Well? You still need to talk?"

He drew a deep breath. "It hurts to talk. I woke up with a sore throat—a bad one."

"Man, I'm sorry." Paige tipped her head back, putting more space between them. "But if you've got some kind of virus, I sure don't want to catch it."

He laughed. "And I don't want you to. I'm trying not to breathe on you or anything."

"Thanks." Slightly relieved, she leaned her head against the window. "So—you wanted to talk about your sore throat?"

"Not exactly."

She lifted her hand, urging him on. "You wanted to talk about . . ."

"My dad." Those two words may not have come easily, but like a cork coming out of a bottle, they released the stream of words that had obviously been swirling around inside him. "RC said I should forgive my dad, so I called the lady at the box office and had two tickets left for him. 'What kind of seats?' she wanted to know, so I told her balcony seats. That way he could see me, but I couldn't see him, you know? She said they were good seats, so I thought I'd done a good thing. But when the bus broke down I started thinking maybe we wouldn't even make this gig and I wouldn't have to deal with him at all, and then I realized I'd be really disappointed if we didn't make it to Las Vegas. One of my reasons is selfish— I think I want Dad to see that I've made it this far without his help."

He had worked himself up, and now he thumped the seat cushion. "Is that so terrible? And I'll admit another thing—I'm curious. I want to know what he looks like; I want to know if he's still anything like the man in the old pictures my mom sent. And if he brings somebody else to the concert—well, maybe I want to know about that, or maybe I don't, I don't know. All I know is if we don't make it to Las Vegas, I'll be really disappointed."

He released a short bark of laughter. "Isn't that, like, the craziest thing you've ever heard? Here I was, dreading this concert and dreading him, but now I'm wishing things were normal and on schedule and these problems hadn't kicked up at all. Most of all . . . I wish I'd reserved front-row seats. I want to look at him. At least I think I do."

He fell silent. When Paige thought he had finished, she lightly touched his shoulder. "You done?"

He exhaled softly. "Yeah."

"Okay, then. Do you want to hear what I really think, or were you just looking for someone to listen to you vent?"

"Um . . . I really want to hear what you think."

She nodded. "I think you're being selfish about everything."

She heard his indrawn gasp.

"Oh yeah," she laughed as she continued, "I know you thought you were being generous by getting him balcony tickets, but you did that to make yourself feel better. You want him to see you and hear you, but from a distance. You don't want him to get too close, and you don't really want him to leave happy . . . am I right?"

She heard a strangled sound come from his throat.

"I know what you're feeling," she went on, leaving him to sort through his thoughts. "My mom left us, too, you know. Dad would disagree, but I think it's because she didn't know what to do with a blind baby, and the thought of taking care of me and Shane and Dad scared her silly. So she ran off to Atlanta, got a job, and now she works in some really tall glass office building. She tells herself her job is hard, but we all know it's not nearly as hard for her as staying with us would have been."

Paige brought her hands together, wishing she could press them to each side of Noah's head and shake some sense into his brain. "You see, Noah, people lie to themselves all the time. You're not so unusual. It happens when we try to figure things out ourselves instead of asking God for help. If we look at things the way Jesus sees them, that's when we get a totally different picture."

Noah didn't speak for a moment, then he cleared his throat. "Okay . . . so what would Jesus do for my dad?"

"Well," she said, slowly choosing her words, "I don't

think he'd stick your dad way up in the balcony. Jesus would want him close, don't you think? And he'd arrange for your dad to have a backstage pass, so you two could visit for a while in the greenroom before the concert starts. And he'd bring gifts—maybe some CDs or posters, but definitely something nice. Something your dad could show his friends after the concert."

Noah snorted softly. "Jesus is one generous guy."

"Yeah, he is. He wants us to love people. And he gives everyone lots of chances to come to him."

"Do you think Jesus would . . . mention my song? I know it's not on the program, but I was thinking maybe Dad heard it on the CMA Awards."

Paige thought a moment, then nodded. "Jesus was always honest, even about uncool things. I think he'd mention your song, but he wouldn't mention it to make your dad feel bad. He'd be honest about the hurt and stuff, but he'd bring up that song so your dad could understand how you found hope by trusting heaven. And who knows? Maybe it will make your father think about God, too."

In a moment of unusual silence without the rumble of the engines or the wail of Larry's country radio, Paige waited to hear his answer.

Finally Noah spoke. "Thanks, Paige," he said, the seat creaking as he stood. "I'll think about what you said."

22

"**MGM Grand Garden Arena.** How may I direct your call?"

"I'd like to speak to Irene, please." Noah looked at his watch. RC had let him use the cell phone with one warning—they needed to conserve power because they might have to call for help if Larry couldn't get the engine bled and the line fixed . . .

"This is Irene. How can I help you?"

"Hi." He turned away from the blinding sun. He'd taken the phone outside for better reception and some privacy. "This is Noah Dudash again, from YB2. Remember me?"

"Well, long time, no talk. Sure I remember you. And we're all real excited about your concert tonight. Everything's sold out, but I managed to snag a couple of tickets for my granddaughter."

"Sold out? But I wanted—well, I'm not sure it'll work, but I wanted to swap those tickets for my dad. Is there any way—any way at all—we can move him from the balcony to the front row on the floor?"

He heard the snap of her gum over the line. "Honey, for *your* dad, I'm sure there's something we can do. After all, they're just chairs."

He exhaled in a rush of relief. "Thanks, Irene. And can you do something else for me?"

"Anything, darlin'."

"Can you leave a couple of backstage passes with those tickets? And maybe a note so he'll know he can come backstage before and after the show."

"Sure thing. I'll slip a couple of all-access passes into his envelope."

"Thanks, Irene."

"You're welcome. And by the way—"

"Yeah?"

"Are you as cute as you sound?"

Noah let out an embarrassed laugh. "I sound cute?"

"Cute as a spotted puppy. But hey, don't worry about me—I'm old enough to be your grandmother. You go on and don't worry about a thing. We'll take care of your Mr. Bill Dudash."

Noah disconnected the call, then slipped the phone into his shirt pocket. Okay, that was settled. Irene would take care of things at the concert hall.

But how were they supposed to get there?

The hands of Larry's dashboard clock had moved halfway around the circle when RC climbed back aboard the bus, his face flushed and sweating.

He dropped into one of the front seats, then nodded at Shane, who sat across from him. "I think we found the problem."

Noah and the others came closer.

"What was it?" Shane asked.

RC mopped sweat from his brow. "A little screw had worked its way loose and punctured a hole in the line. But Larry's patching the line now, and we should make it to the nearest gas station. They'll make a permanent repair there, so we should soon be on our way to Las Vegas."

RC turned and looked toward the back of the bus, his

eyes darting from seat to seat as if he were counting heads. "Is everybody up?"

"Yeah," Shane answered. "Joe's back there writing a letter, but he's awake."

"Good. Gather everybody around the tables, will you, while I go back and wash up. I'd like to talk to you all as we head into Vegas."

RC stood and made his way to the bathroom. Noah and the others let him pass through the narrow aisle, then they moved to the center section where two tables faced each other. Liane and Paige slid into the first table, while Noah, Shane, and Josiah sat at the opposite one. Taz had gone outside to help Larry, and RC probably wanted him to stay there—Larry could use all the help he could get.

Josiah wore the look of a kid who thinks he's in serious trouble. "What's this all about? We don't usually meet on the bus."

Shane shrugged. "Don't worry. We're going to be arriving late, so Dad probably wants to have our group time now."

"I think he wants us to pray we make it to Vegas," Liane quipped. "Have you ever been in a mechanic's shop? Sometimes they can take *hours* to do the simplest thing."

"It's not going to take hours," Paige said, her voice flat. "We're going to make it on time without any hassle. I think God wants us to play in Vegas tonight."

"Why?" Shane sputtered a laugh. "So we can distract all the gamblers for a couple of hours?"

She tilted her head and curved her mouth in a small, secret smile. "Maybe God has his reasons."

Noah closed his eyes, then looked down at the table-top. He knew Paige was thinking about his dad. She believed God wanted them to reach Vegas so Noah could meet his father.

"Thanks, guys, for gathering around." RC came through the narrow doorway that led to the bunks, then sank into an empty space on the bench where the girls had gathered. "I thought we'd take a few minutes to talk and pray before we get on the road—*if* we get on the road. Larry's assured me we'll make it, but I'd rather get a little assurance from above, if you know what I mean."

Noah relaxed as RC's easy smile played over the group. "Now." RC dropped his hands on the table. "I wanted to talk to you today about one of the secrets for getting along as a group. This morning, as I was outside helping Larry look for the problem with the bus, I found myself growing irritated with him—oh, I know it was an acci-dent, but I kept thinking, 'Why doesn't Larry carry a spare line?' and 'Why hasn't he maintained this engine better?' Now, I was off base in my thoughts because there's no way Larry could know what was going to happen, but I let the pressure of the moment get to me—and I was beginning to get to Larry."

RC's smile broadened. "That's when Larry asked me to send Taz out to help him. Taz wouldn't be judgmental, you see. I was beginning to drive Larry crazy."

A scattering of smiles showed on the faces around the

group. Noah knew they all thought RC was a great guy, but sometimes in rehearsal, especially when they were tired and not performing to the best of their ability, he could drive anyone crazy.

"The other day I was reading a book about animals," RC went on. "Did you know that in the highest Pyrenees mountains there's a breed of mountain goat so rare the animals are hardly ever seen? The old goats always keep companions—young goats that follow them around. The young goats sound a warning if enemies ever appear, and all the mountain goats—young and old—get away."

His gaze softened as his eyes fell upon Josiah. "There's more than one lesson in that story—not only do the goats teach us that there's value in teamwork, it also demonstrates that those who have been around the longest can still benefit from newcomers."

"I'd like to share one more animal story. There's a badger-like creature called the ratel, and in nature it teams up with the honeyguide bird. The little bird spies the honey and leads the way to it, then the ratel's sharp claws are able to tear into the hive so both the bird and the beast can enjoy the honey."[1]

"I feel sorry for the bees," Noah quipped. RC grinned. "Now—who can guess why I'm telling you these animal stories?"

Paige lifted her hand. "Cooperation," she said, sounding faintly bored. "You want us to cooperate with each other."

"You guys have always cooperated great. But what can

get in the way of that?" When no one answered immediately, RC's eyes narrowed and seemed to focus on Noah.

"Uh," Noah said, feeling singled out, "trouble? When, like, someone says something to someone else and feelings get hurt?"

RC nodded. "That's right. When one person does something to hurt a friend, mutual cooperation can go right out the door. And on a team as small as ours, one broken link can spell disaster for us all."

Noah frowned as he looked around the circle. Had one of them done something to hurt someone else? He hadn't noticed any arguing or pouting, so what was RC getting at?

RC must have noticed his searching look. "Sometimes," he continued, his voice earnest, "we can bring a problem from the outside into the group . . . and when we dwell on it, that situation begins to affect everything we are and everything we do. That's when we realize we have to deal with it . . . and usually that means we have to forgive whoever hurt us. We have to forgive because Jesus forgave us."

Noah lowered his head as the meaning behind RC's words became clear. He didn't know what sort of problems the others were dealing with, but RC had to be talking about the situation with Noah and his dad. But hadn't he already chosen to forgive? He'd gotten the man tickets to the concert and arranged for backstage passes. What more did he have to do?

"I just want you to keep these things in mind as we

go out to perform tonight." RC rapped his knuckles on the table. "And when we arrive at the loading dock, I'll need all of you to hit the ground running. Guys, give Taz a hand at the soundboard if you can, and girls, be quick in the changing rooms. It'd help if you could lay out the guys' outfits so they won't have to search for costume changes between sets."

Paige and Liane nodded.

"One more thing." RC snapped his fingers. "Noah, I'd like you and Paige to perform 'I'm Trusting Heaven' again between the first and second sets. Think you can handle that?"

Noah lifted his head. "I've got a sore throat, RC. It feels terrible."

"But can you sing?"

The question hung in the air, unanswered, and Noah's gaze flew to Paige's face. He couldn't tell what she was thinking, but he thought he saw her lips part in a small smile.

Could he push past the pain to sing that song with his dad in the audience? The man might not show up, but then again, he might.

"You sure?" he croaked, looking at RC.

The director nodded. "I've given it a lot of thought, and I think you need to sing that song tonight."

After a moment of indecision, Noah agreed.

24

Larry sweet-talked the bus into making it to Mesquite, a small town on the Nevada state line, where they pulled into a garage. There RC did a little sweet-talking of his own, convincing the mechanic to stop what he was doing in order to fix the vehicle. As an added incentive, the singers handed out glossy auto-graphed photos to the handful of customers sitting in the garage's waiting room—one elderly man, a woman with a red-haired toddler, and two men who wore overalls and didn't talk much.

An hour later YB2 was rolling down Interstate 15, almost to Las Vegas. Noah was no longer worried about whether they'd make it to Vegas; now his energy went into worrying about how he would sing his song in front of his father. He'd had a hard time getting through both

Noah

verses at the CMA. Would he be able to sing it with his dad sitting only a few feet away?

He was glad when he looked up to see Paige standing in the aisle next to his seat. "Mind if I join you?"

"No." He slid closer toward the window to make room, then shifted to face her. "I'm glad you came over. I was getting a little nervous about our song tonight."

"We'll get there in plenty of time to rehearse. And I'm sure you'll do fine."

He lifted one shoulder in a shrug. "Maybe. But I'll be nervous. Probably more nervous than I was the other night in Nashville."

She smiled beneath her glasses. "You'll do fine—just sing from your heart. I know this will be a special night for you, since your dad's coming and all."

"*Might* be—I'm not sure he will."

"Oh, I think he will." She hesitated a moment. "About what my dad said—Noah, I need to ask you something."

"Yeah? Ask away."

"Have I—I mean—well, I've been wondering." Her brows dashed down to hide beneath her glasses, then lifted again. "Have I done anything lately to make you mad at me? You've been acting different, and I need to know . . ."

He closed his eyes as truth and kindness butted heads in his brain. Man, why did girls like to talk so much about their *feelings?*

"You haven't done anything, Paige," he said, choosing kindness.

"Really? Well . . . that's good. So if I didn't do anything, you've been avoiding me for some reason of your own, then."

He snorted. "Have I been avoiding you?"

"Yes, you have. When you come on the bus you say hi to Joe and Liane, then pass over me as if I'm invisible. Just because I can't see you doesn't mean you can't see me. I learned that lesson when I was five years old."

Shaking his head, Noah resorted to truth. "Well— okay. To be perfectly honest—"

"I like honesty."

"Good. Because when Liane told me you had a crush on me, I didn't want to believe it. But I started thinking she might be right, and I didn't want to do anything to encourage you—because of the rules, you know. So . . . yeah, maybe I have been avoiding you a little. But only because I didn't want to hurt you."

"Liane told you *what?*"

"She said . . . that she thought maybe you liked me . . . you know, as more than a friend."

"Oh, Noah." She sounded hurt and turned her head away.

"Okay," she finally said, resting her head on her hand, "I'll admit that ever since that day in the elevator, I've thought of you in a different way. I had never really spent much time alone with you before, and that night you seemed . . . well, pretty cool."

He opened his mouth, about to answer her compliment

with a wisecrack, then realized this was not the time
for jokes.

It was time to be embarrassed.

"Man." He whispered the word, then turned his face
toward the window, grateful she couldn't see the blush
scorching his neck.

"I know the rules, too, Noah, and I would never have
put any pressure on you—well, to be a couple or anything. I only wanted to . . . enjoy our friendship. You
always seemed to be such good friends with Lee; I wanted
that with you, too."

"Wow, Paige." He rolled his eyes, searching for words.
"I do like you a lot. As a friend."

"That's all I want to hear." She patted his hand as a
sister would, then crossed her arms. "I was jealous of Lee,
and that was bad—and I need to apologize for being rude
to both of you. But if you and I can agree to be friends,
then I'll be happy. That's all I want, Noah. Your friendship
means a lot to me."

"That's cool." Not knowing what else to do, he nudged
her shoulder. "You bet. And thanks, Paige."

"You're welcome."

She sighed, leaning back heavily in the chair. "Wow.
Dad was right. I feel so much better now that I've come
clean with you about this."

Noah stared at her. "You talked to RC about all of
this?"

She blew out a breath. "No, but isn't it obvious he
saw everything? I ought to apologize to everybody, 'cause

I know this morning's devotion had my name written all over it. I was aggravated with you and Lee, and it affected the group." A blush colored the tops of her cheekbones. "I'm just glad RC didn't correct me in front of everyone. I'd have absolutely *died* if this came out before I had a chance to talk to you."

She tapped him on the knee, then stood and moved to the back of the bus.

Left alone with his thoughts, Noah chewed on his thumbnail and smiled to himself. He could have sworn RC's devotion was directed only at him, but Paige had thought their early morning talk was about her.

Funny . . . maybe everyone had stuff to work out.

25

Paige caught Liane in the dressing room. "Thanks a lot, Lee. And you call yourself a friend?"

"What?"

"Thanks for telling Noah that I was crazy in love with him."

"I did not tell him you were in love with him." Liane's voice rang with indignation. "I told him you'd been talking about him in your sleep. And you had, Paige. Every night."

"So? I probably talk about all the guys."

"Not like this. Admit it—you like him."

"Maybe I did—but you and I both know that's not a good idea."

"Exactly. That's why I told Noah to be careful. I didn't want him to hurt your feelings."

"So you embarrassed me instead?"

"Paige." Liane's voice softened. "I didn't mean to embarrass you. I thought I was doing you a favor."

"Well, you didn't." Paige crossed her arms. "And the next time you're tempted to tell one of my secrets, talk to me before you go blabbing to everyone else, okay?"

The room filled with silence, then Liane whispered, "I'm sorry."

Paige drew a deep breath. She'd been hurt and humiliated when Noah talked to her, but she couldn't stay mad at Liane. In a group as small as YB2, it was never a good idea to let anger last for too long.

"It's okay, Lee, I forgive you," she finally said. "But the next time I talk in my sleep . . . wake me up, will you?"

26

At precisely 8:10 p.m., the lights of the MGM Grand
Garden Arena flashed, the speakers roared with the sound
of rockets in flight, and artificial fog poured across the
platform. The lights went dark, and Noah's heart pounded
as YB2 ran to their marks on the stage.

They had made it to Las Vegas. Everything had been
a little crazy when they arrived behind schedule, but RC
and Taz had quickly set things in order.

And a ten-minute delay was nothing compared to the
disaster they could have faced.

Although his throat was still a little sore, Noah con-
centrated on the music and his dance movements as he
sang the first verse of their opening number. Only during
a three-measure instrumental interlude did he dare to
scan the front row of floor seats for a man who might be
his father.

He had provided tickets and all-access passes, but no one resembling his dad had come backstage before the concert. No one had left him a phone message; no one had sent a note.

Okay, then. He could relax and treat this like an ordinary concert. He had stewed over it for nothing. His father hadn't even cared enough to come.

But on the third chorus, when the group ran down the ramps and into the audience, Noah followed Liane into the center front section and saw a balding man standing motionless amid a group of screaming, jumping teenage girls. Like the girls, the man held a hand-lettered sign, but he held it tightly beneath a quivering chin and cheeks that streamed with tears.

His father.

Something in Noah broke at the sight. Shouldering his way through the screaming girls, Noah ran over to the man . . . and in those faded blue eyes he saw the father he'd seen in his mom's old photos. With only a few seconds to spare, Noah wrapped the man in a brief embrace, then obeyed the pounding music and returned to the stage.

It was only during the song's final note that Noah caught the meaning behind the man's simple sign: We ♥ Noah Dudash.

Sweaty and jittery, Noah had just bent over the water fountain in the hall outside the men's dressing room when a male voice fell upon his ear. "Noah? I wanted to thank you for the tickets. The concert was . . . wonderful."

Noah whirled around. His father and a young blonde girl stood slightly off to the side. The girl, who looked to be about eleven or twelve, wore the dizzy expression of most girls at a YB2 concert. But the man—his dad—was focused on Noah's face.

"Dad?" Noah wiped his mouth with his sleeve, then thrust out his hand. "Thank you for coming. I wasn't sure you would."

"I wouldn't miss it. I'm sorry we were late, but Julie here—" he gestured to the girl—"had piano lessons tonight. Her mom wouldn't let her miss." He shrugged. "You know all about music lessons, I guess."

Noah nodded. "I do."

"Hey, Noah." The girl just stared at him.

"Hey there, Julie." Noah gave her a brief smile, then returned his attention to his father. Who was this kid, and why had she tagged along to this father-and-son reunion?

"Julie," his dad said, "is Joan's daughter."

Noah tilted his head. "Who's Joan?"

"She's my wife." His father cleared his throat. "We've been married about three years. She works at a casino on the Strip."

Noah nodded, then glanced toward the dressing room. He'd already heard more than he wanted to know, and he was rapidly running out of things to say. His mom would ask about what his dad had said, and he didn't want to have to tell her things about a new wife and a new kid . . .

"Listen, Son," his dad said as he looked at his watch, "this is a school night for Julie, so I promised to get her home at a decent hour. But it was good to see you. I'm proud of you, Son, and I'm sure your mom is proud of you, too. The next time you come through town, you be sure to give me a holler and we'll sit down and have coffee or something."

"Sure, Dad."

Noah stared at his father as a geyser of emotions rose within him. Despite the sign and the tears he'd seen earlier, apparently his dad wasn't interested in getting to know him. He might have come tonight out of simple curiosity, or maybe he promised this girl free tickets to a YB2 concert.

But he obviously didn't want a relationship with Noah . . . at least nothing that went deeper than exchanging hellos every few years. Or maybe he did want a relationship and didn't know how to start one after all this time.

But that was okay. What had Paige said? God wants us to love people . . . and he gives lots of chances for them to come to him.

Noah could give his father a chance, too.

"You know, Dad," Noah said, leaning one hand against the painted wall, "I want you to know something."

His father's eyes narrowed slightly. "Yeah?"

"That song Paige and I sang together—I wrote that about you. I wrote it about the hurt you caused when you went away, and the hurt I still feel because you're out of my life. But I want you to know this—I forgive you for everything, and I'll keep on forgiving you as long as I live. You'll always be my father."

Noah watched as his dad's chin quivered enough to bristle the stubble on his cheek, then he nodded and took the girl's hand.

"Before you go," Noah said, taking a step toward the dressing room, "would you like a free CD? a T-shirt? I've got a whole bag of YB2 stuff picked out for you."

The girl's eyes lit up, but his dad only gripped her

hand more firmly and shook his head. Without another word he waved, then turned and walked away.

Noah stood there, watching him, until he heard a soft voice by his side.

"That your dad leaving?"

"Uh-huh." He narrowed his eyes as the man and girl disappeared into the crowd of crew members. "How'd you know?"

Paige shrugged. "Smells—tobacco and chewing gum. Who was the kid?"

"His new wife's daughter."

"Oh." Paige said nothing, but after a moment she linked her arm through Noah's. "You okay?"

"Yeah." Noah straightened. "Yeah, I am. Really."

Her brow arched as she smiled. "Walk me to the girls' dressing room?"

Noah looked down the hall, where his father and the girl had disappeared. Maybe forgiveness did come at a price, but this feeling of freedom was worth it.

"Any time, Paige," he said, taking her arm as he led the way.

I'm Trusting Heaven

I thought life would sorta flow by,
I never had much reason to cry,
Until you left me alone.
I thought I'd caught the golden ring,
Life offered me so many things,
Until my heart turned to stone.

Chorus:
Now now now, I'm trusting heaven alone,
Now I'm thinkin' 'bout another home,
Now I'm trading in my heart of stone,
I'm trusting heaven . . . heaven alone.

We always walked together down by the shore,
I gave you my heart, you're the one I adored,
Until you said 'so long.'

Noah

You were the only one I could always trust,
But when you left, oh something told me I must
Look toward something else . . .

Chorus:
Now now now, I'm trusting heaven alone,
Now I'm thinkin' 'bout another home,
Now I'm trading in my heart of stone,
I'm trusting heaven . . . heaven alone.

Maybe you never meant to hurt me,
Maybe the future's dark and murky,
Maybe you never would desert me,
But I still miss you . . .

Chorus:
Now now now, I'm trusting heaven alone,
Now I'm thinkin' 'bout another home,
Now I'm trading in my heart of stone,
I'm trusting heaven . . . heaven alone.

WORDS AND MUSIC BY NOAH DUDASH,
ARRANGED BY PAIGE CLAWSON, 2003.

Young Believer™ ON TOUR

Collect all 6 books in the Young Believer on Tour series!

 **1 Josiah**

 **2 Liane**

 **3 Noah**

 **4 Paige**

 **5 Shane**

 **6 Taz**

youngbeliever.com

NEVER STOP BELIEVING!

Have you ever wondered why Christians believe what they do? Or how you're supposed to figure out *what* to believe? Maybe you hear words and phrases and it seems like you're supposed to know what they mean. If you've ever thought about this stuff, then the *Young Believer Bible* is for you! There isn't another Bible like it.

The *Young Believer Bible* will help you understand what the Bible is about, what Christians believe, and how to act on what you've figured out. With dozens of "Can You Believe It?" and "That's a Fact!" notes that tell of the many crazy, miraculous, and hard-to-believe events in the Bible, hundreds of "Say What??" definitions of Christian words you'll hear people talk about, plus many more cool features, you will learn why it's important to . . . **Never stop believing!**

Ready for more?

Other items available in the Young Believer product line:

Young Believer Case Files

Be sure to check out
www.youngbeliever.com

How easy is it to live out your faith?

Sometimes it may seem as though no one is willing to stand up for God today. Well, *Young Believer Case Files* is here to prove that's simply not true!

Meet a group of young believers who had the guts to live out their Christian faith. Some of them had to make tough decisions, others had to hold on to God's promises during sickness or some other loss, and still others found courage to act on what God says is right, even when other people disagreed.

You can have the kind of powerful faith that makes a difference in your own life and in the lives of people around you.

The question is . . . how will YOU live out your faith?

Young Believer 365

Be sure to check out
www.youngbeliever.com

365?? You mean every day??
You'd better believe it!

Maybe you know something about the Bible . . . or maybe you don't. Maybe you know what Christians believe . . . or maybe it's new to you. It's impossible to know everything about the Bible and Christianity because God always has more to show us in his Word. *Young Believer 365* is a great way to learn more about who God is and what he's all about.

Through stories, Scripture verses, and ideas for how to live out your faith, this book will help you grow as a young believer. Experience God's power each day as you learn more about God's amazing love, his awesome plans, and his incredible promises for you.

Start today. See what God has in store for you!

Never stop believing!

WheRe AdvEnture beGins with a BoOk!

LoG oN @
Cool2Read.com

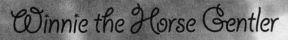

Winnie the Horse Gentler Series:

Collect all eight books!

www.winniethehorsegentler.com

Get to know Winnie and Lizzy, plus all of their friends, horses, and more at winniethehorsegentler.com!

Check out all these fun features:

★ Post your own stories and photos of your pet

★ Trivia games

★ Articles by the author

★ Advice on pet care

★ And much more!

MARS
DIARIES
are you ready?

Set in an experimental community on Mars in the years 2039–2043, the Mars Diaries feature teen virtual-reality specialist Tyce Sanders. Life on the red planet is not always easy, but it is definitely exciting. As Tyce explores his strange surroundings, he also finds that the mysteries of the planet point to his greatest discovery—a new relationship with God.

MISSION 1: OXYGEN LEVEL ZERO
Time was running out...

MISSION 2: ALIEN PURSUIT
"Help me!" And the radio went dead....

MISSION 3: TIME BOMB
A quake rocks the red planet, uncovering a long kept secret....

MISSION 4: HAMMERHEAD
I was dead center in the laser target controls....

MISSION 5: SOLE SURVIVOR
Scientists buried alive at cave-in site!

MISSION 6: MOON RACER
Everyone has a motive...and secrets. The truth must be found before it's too late.

MISSION 7: COUNTDOWN
20 soldiers, 20 neuron rifles. There was nowhere to run. Nowhere to hide...

MISSION 8: ROBOT WAR
Ashley and I are their only hope, and they think we're traitors.

MISSION 9: MANCHURIAN SECTOR
I was in trouble...and I couldn't trust anyone.

MISSION 10: LAST STAND
Invasion was imminent ... and we'd lost all contact with Earth.

Visit Tyce on-line!

- ○ Learn more about the red planet from a real expert
- ○ Great contests and awesome prizes
- ○ Fun quizzes and games
- ○ Find out when the next book is coming out

Discover the latest news about the Mars Diaries.
Visit www.marsdiaries.com